She laughed shakily to herself. There must be a great dusty mirror at the end of this corridor, that they hadn't noticed in the dark, before. Fancy being about to scream at her own stupid reflection!

Except . . . the dark shape behind the flame in the mirror seemed much bigger than her; the pale blur of the face much higher up. Was it a trick mirror that made you look tall, like they had in fairgrounds?

Another stab below warned her to get on. But, as she raised a foot, the figure in the mirror seemed to move towards her. She put her own foot back abruptly. But the figure in the mirror kept on moving towards her. Got bigger and bigger. Far taller than she was. She could see long pale fingers now, cupped round the flame. And the face had a dark cowl round it, and a touch of white at the throat that had nothing to do with her own red T-shirt. And it was draped to its feet in black, with just a flicker where the feet were moving. And the face was a woman's face, with long thin nose and pursed lips and huge dark eyes . . .

Also by Robert Westall:

BREAK OF DARK

GHOST ABBEY

robert
WESTALL

Corgi Books

GHOST ABBEY
A CORGI BOOK 9780552568760

First published in Great Britain simultaneously by
Macmillan Publishers Ltd and Hippo Books, 1988

Corgi edition published 2004

5 7 9 10 8 6 4

Copyright © The Estate of Robert Westall, 1988

The right of Robert Westall to be identified as the author of this work has been
asserted in accordance with the Copyright, Designs and Patents Act 1988.

Set in 11.5/16.5pt Sabon by
Falcon Oast Graphic Art Ltd.

Corgi Books are published by Random House Children's Books,
61–63 Uxbridge Road, London W5 5SA
a division of The Random House Group Ltd.

Addresses for companies within The Random House Group Limited
can be found at:
www.randomhouse.co.uk/offices.htm.

THE RANDOM HOUSE GROUP Limited Reg. No. 954009
www.kidsatrandomhouse.co.uk

A CIP catalogue record for this book is available from the British Library.

The Random House Group Limited supports The Forest Stewardship
Council® (FSC®), the leading international forest-certification organisation.
Our books carrying the FSC label are printed on FSC®-certified paper.
FSC is the only forest-certification scheme supported by the leading
environmental organisations, including Greenpeace. Our
paper procurement policy can be found at
www.randomhouse.co.uk/environment

Printed and bound in Great Britain by Clays Ltd, St Ives plc

*In memory of Maggie, my mother,
and her beloved father, George Leggett,
master-builder*

CHAPTER 1

Maggi struggled up the hill, swapping her bulging briefcase from hand to hand every five yards. Why did she leave everything in her desk till the last day of term?

The heat made the handle slippery. Being thin, she wasn't used to sweating. But this summer was so hot that even the boys who played footie non-stop in the yard all year round were lying on the stone floors in the school corridors, trying to get cool.

Stubbings Hill stretched up before her, like the Sahara. Worse, because the baking red brick threw back the heat, making the narrow terrace like an oven. Every time she crossed the road to get into a sliver of shade, the melting tar-bubbles sucked at her feet.

It was nearly as lonely as the Sahara too. All the shadowed front doors were open, to catch the merest breath of air; the curtains of every open window were drawn against the sun, so she seemed to walk through an endless funeral. But there wasn't a breath of air; not even the thinnest curtain moved an inch.

Still, she wasn't too hot to forget the potatoes at the corner shop. If she forgot, she had to go back. There was no one else to do it, since Mam died.

'By gum, hinny, you look meltin',' said Mr Johnson sympathetically. 'If I see that bag o' yours lying next to a big grease spot on the pavement, Aah'll know ye *have* melted!'

She had to smile. Normally he was so neat in his white coat. But this weather he'd changed into a floppy yellow T-shirt that clashed badly with his turkey-red neck. And he was wearing his khaki shorts from the Western Desert; the ones he'd seen off Rommel in. They came down below his knees. To meet red socks pulled up over blue trainers. If Mr Johnson had looked like that in the Western Desert, no wonder Rommel had run!

He banged down a five-pound bag of potatoes. 'Fifty-five to you, little missus!'

She shot a sharp look at the rack in the corner, where the potatoes were kept. But they really were fifty-five, to anybody.

Everybody might know their family was hard-up. But she wouldn't take charity. Mam wouldn't have stood for taking charity. She pulled her purse out of her blazer, and counted out the fifty-five in small change; suddenly terrified she wouldn't have enough, though she'd counted it twice already.

'Tek care!!' warned Mr Johnson. 'Aah'll keep an eye open for that grease spot!'

She hefted the potatoes in one hand, and her brief-case in the other; grimaced a grin because the weight pulled back her lips into a snarl, and left.

'Eeh,' said Mrs Johnson, from where she was stacking bottles of bitter lemon in the back room. 'She's a real little housewife that one. Doesn't miss a trick.'

'Not natural, in a kid of twelve.'

'Who else is there to do it?'

'I thought her dad paid Doreen Streeton . . .'

'Doreen Streeton!'

The contempt in his wife's voice silenced Mr Johnson for a moment. Then he said, to console himself, 'Maggi's a real little worker – just like her mum – never stops.'

'It's a pity her mam hadn't stopped sometimes. Dyin' wi' her heart at thirty-five . . .'

Faced with such tragedy, all Mr Johnson could think of was to go into the back of the shop for a crate of Coke he didn't need.

Rage seized Maggi the moment she turned the corner and saw her house. The only one without curtains drawn against the sun; the only one with no open doors or windows. The place would be unbearable for Dad coming home; unbearable till midnight. And it would make the twins ratty, and they'd bicker all evening and not go to sleep when they went to bed. Dad would get no peace.

She *hated* Mrs Streeton; even more when she opened the door with her latchkey and saw the yellow plastic bucket, full of cold dirty water, halfway up the half-washed tiled floor of the hall. The mop was still stuck in it; the mop-head was falling to bits already from too much soaking. And the whole lot was placed just where the twins, gallumping downstairs, would fall over it and send it flying.

Maggi looked up at the hall light-fitting. The thin black cobwebs still trailed from it, like they always did. Mrs Streeton had never been known to lift her arm above her shoulder. So the picture rails never got dusted till they looked like they'd been covered by a black snowstorm.

And the bits of the hall floor that had been washed hadn't been dried, were still sopping wet, so you could slip and break your neck.

And Mrs Streeton would be sitting at the kitchen table with the radio on, a third mug of tea in front of her, taking her interminable afternoon break.

Mrs Streeton was there as forecast. If it had been Dad coming in, Mrs Streeton would have been lying back in her chair, displaying her opulent bosom. Mrs Streeton always sat back when Dad was around. But as it was just Maggi, she sat forward. And the usual fag in her mouth, and at least five lipstick-stained fag-ends screwed up tight and mean in the ashtray. Some tea-break! And her skirt was too short as usual. And her flashy legs in their high-heeled court shoes with no tights, as usual. And the kitchen sink was still full of the breakfast washing-up, onto which the hot tap dripped musically and wastefully.

Mrs Streeton pushed back her streak-dyed hair nervously, under Maggi's glare, and went onto the offensive.

'There's nothing for his tea, you know. I've looked in the fridge an' there's only some old tomatoes.'

Maggi waved the bag of potatoes triumphantly.

'We got bangers an' mash wi' the tomatoes.'

'Bangers?' Mrs Streeton seemed ever so slightly flustered. 'I found a few bangers . . . I had them for me lunch. I had to have something . . . your dad said I was always to get myself something . . . but there weren't *many* – look!'

She pulled a blood-stained plate out of the fridge. Five limp pale bangers still flopped on it. All that was left of a carefully calculated three-quarters of a pound.

Maggi could've wept. Instead she shouted.

'You've eaten our *tea*. All there *was* . . .'

'Don't get shirty wi' me. How was I to know? Them bangers'd be *nothing* in a house wi' a proper mother. That's what you kids need – a proper mam. A nice feller like your dad shouldn't have to struggle on, on his own . . .'

'A proper mam like *you*, I suppose. Always asking him to meet you at the Collingwood Arms, when you know he can't afford to drink!'

'Your dad needs a bit o' fun!'

Maggi just looked at her, from head to foot. Could her dad ever see any fun in *that*? There was a roll of fat below the big bosom. The legs were mottled by being close to the fire too often. The high-heeled shoes were scuffed, hadn't seen a lick of polish since they were bought. Mam had been as neat as a pin.

But Maggi couldn't understand what men *saw* in Doris Streeton . . . what Dad might see. Five gold rings; and dirty fingernails.

Their eyes locked; nobody said anything. Nobody had any need to say anything.

Then Mrs Streeton said, 'Don't be impertinent with me, young woman. Or you'll feel my hand across your face . . .'

But they both knew she wouldn't *dare*.

Maggi reached up to the kitchen mantelpiece, and took down a sealed envelope. 'Here's your money for the week, Mrs Streeton. Dad won't be home till late.'

She enjoyed the way the woman's face fell; the way she gathered up her bits and pieces with drooping shoulders, and banged the front door as she left.

Maggi didn't enjoy clearing up the mess she'd left behind; opening the doors and windows and drawing the curtains, in a too-late attempt to cool the house. She didn't enjoy trailing down to the Post Office either, to draw the last three pounds out of her own savings, to buy more sausages with. But if the twins weren't fed till Dad got home, they'd tear the house apart.

It was only then she saw the letter. Mrs Streeton had bunged it on the hall table, upside down. The letter was so big she thought it must be an offer. She enjoyed offers; they contained marvellous coloured photographs of beautiful holidays and yachts and homes; she always read them from cover to cover, before shoving them in the bin.

But this wasn't an offer. The envelope was rich and creamy, with a pattern in the shine of it. It felt like a different world, with big black cars that didn't belong to undertakers, and afternoon tea served on silver trays.

Best of all, it was addressed to: 'George R. Adams, FTC'. Her father's full title, when everyone else referred to him as 'Little Geordie Adams', or even 'poor Geordie Adams'. And it wasn't a bill, because it was written in the most marvellous spiky, flowing, arrogant writing, that threatened to leap off the paper and run about the room like a spider. The postmark was Cheshire. Cheshire cheese. Cows. Green fields . . . a vision of glory filled Maggi. She just somehow knew the letter was terribly, terribly important. And that it was terribly important that Dad read the letter in peace, without the twins pestering him.

At which point the twins arrived back from school. Looking thin and long-legged and malevolent as spiders, in their washed-out jeans. Flaxen haired, high as kites with the freedom of the holidays, and ready for trouble!

But she still had one pound seventy-six of her money. And only one thing would get rid of the twins in this mood.

'Wanta go to the baths?'

They looked hopeful, but said together, 'No money!'

'I'll treat you.'

'What's the catch?' they said together.

'Your bedroom tidied. IMMACULATE! An' the table laid. IMMACULATE!'

That had been Mam's favourite word. Immaculate.

'Bedroom,' said Baz.

'Table,' said Gaz. They found little need for words.

In half an hour, they were fed and gone. She called after them, 'You needn't hurry back. Nine o'clock.'

She still had a pound left. She nipped out for a can

of Dad's favourite lager, and put it in the fridge to get really cold.

Dad pushed back his plate, with a sigh of satisfaction.

'By, that was smashin', hinny.' He always said that after every meal she cooked; even when she'd burnt something. As he'd always said it to Mam.

Then she brought him his lager, and the pint pot he'd pinched from the pub as a lad. Its knobbles were dulled and scratched with the years, but it was precious to him. He looked younger when he picked it up and drank a third, and watched the foam slide back down the side.

'Is this on the housekeeping? By, ye've made it stretch like elastic this week!' That was another thing he'd always said to Mam.

Maggi said nothing; just produced the letter from where she'd hidden it safe under the plastic tablecloth.

He looked worried, until he realized it wasn't a bill. But she could tell he was pleased to see the letters after his name. Then he took a clean knife from the kitchen drawer, and slit it open, as carefully as everything his clever fingers did.

She watched his face as he read. Two years ago, she'd thought him the handsomest dad in the school. His moustache was clipped short then, his hair short-back-and-sides, like the soldier he'd once been. But since Mam died, the moustache had grown longer, and drooped like a sickly plant. His blond hair had grown long, and curled up at the back; and there was a little white bald patch showing under the hair in the middle of his head. And there were wrinkly bags under his kind lost blue eyes. She could've wept that two years could've made such a difference. Mrs Streeton had been right about one thing. Poor Geordie Adams didn't have much fun in his life.

His brow wrinkled. 'Edward St Germaine, architect? Aah divven't knaa any Edward St Germaine!' Then he suddenly laughed, and looked like a boy again. 'Aah've got him! He called hisself plain Ted German in those days! To us lads, anyway. He was quite one o' the lads himself.' He looked at Maggi, and the years seemed to have dropped off him. 'A mad feller, he was. Aah went to work for him in London, after Aah left the army. Afore Aah met yer mam. Shop-fitting in the King's Road and Carnaby Street. We'd move in on a Saturday night, rip the old shop apart, and have the new shop ready for Monday morning. Thirty-six hours, non-stop. Aah used to smoke sixty fags a day, then. Light one up, put it down, and by the time you looked for it again, it was burnt out. After we'd finished, we'd get a bit of kip, get washed an' shaved, and then go on the town for a good night out. Nothin' to do but booze – we were livin' in digs, four to a rabbit-hutch. Money was good though – double time, and treble time for Sundays. A week's pay in thirty-six hours. Aah was his foreman then . . . kept the wild ones at it. Aah earned enough money, on the lump, to buy this house an' marry yer mam and set up in business for meself!'

Then his blue eyes clouded, remembering Mam.

'What does . . . Ted German . . . want?' asked Maggi quickly, to get the agony out of his eyes.

'He wants me as foreman again. He's doin' up a stately home in Cheshire. He's come up in the world, has Ted German. But his usual foreman's fell off a scaffold an' broken both his legs, and he can't get a good man.'

'Will you go?' Maggi's eyes had gone very wide. A stately home; like Seaton Delaval, where she'd gone on a trip with the school . . . statues and paintings . . . and Cheshire cheese and green fields and cows and . . .

The laughing young man in front of her crumpled again into her worried old dad. 'What, leave this house? Wi' all the burglars an' vandals aboot?'

But she knew it wasn't the house. He couldn't care less about the house. There were four slates loose he'd been promising to see to since last winter. No, he just didn't want to make the effort. He'd just drifted along since Mam died. Mending roofs for old ladies who couldn't afford to pay him the right price. Mending broken windows for Social Services, who didn't pay him for months. When once he'd built whole houses. All he seemed to want to do these days was make enough money to get by, and then settle in front of the telly for the evening, with a can of lager, watching any old thing that came on, whether he was interested or not. Often he fell asleep over the telly, and its whining sounds would bring her downstairs, and she'd find him gaping and snoring over a grey screen.

Just drifting. And drifting towards Doris Streeton. Better men than Dad had married worse than Doris Streeton, just to get their shirts washed . . .

'Dad,' she said desperately, 'it'd be a new start for you!'

For some reason, he took her seriously. 'But we'd have to live all on our own in that big house. You'd have nobody to help you. Aall the cookin' an' aall the washin' . . . Aah can't ask a bairn of twelve to do that. An' you'd have to go to new schools . . . an' the job's only for a year . . .'

'I'll manage. I'm nearly thirteen. If we don't like it, we can come back when school starts in September. It can be like a holiday.'

He looked guilty. They'd had a holiday every year when Mam was alive. Camping holidays. They'd never had one since.

She pressed home her advantage.

'Honestly, Dad, the twins will kick this place apart if we stay here. I can't control them any more – they're getting too big. They'll drive me mad. In Cheshire they'll have trees an' fields. I *can* manage, Dad, honestly. If we're going on holiday, the twins will help. You can make Gaz promise . . .'

Dad was looking at her, with that dazed and dreamy expression on his face he sometimes got when they argued. She knew what he was going to say before he said it.

'Eeh, Maggi, you look just like your mam when you want something bad. You're the spittin' image of her.' He picked up his knife and drew patterns in the congealing grease of his plate. 'Ted German's offering good money. Though Aah've never heard of the charity he's workin' for – the Marigold Trust . . .'

'Have they got the money to pay you?'

'Eeh, that's your mam talkin' too. Aye, Ted German'll see me right. But it'll be rough, pet. The house has been empty for years. He doesn't even say if there's any furniture.'

'We've got all the camping stuff in the attic.'

'Aah suppose Aah could ask Mrs Streeton to keep an eye on the house while we're gone . . .'

'*No*,' she said, very definitely. 'Old Mr Sanders next

door'll see to it. He won't charge you. You can bring him some fags for a present.'

A knowing smile crept across his face. As if he'd just made some great discovery. 'Aah reckon you're not over-fond of Mrs Streeton, our Maggi.'

She just looked at him.

'Eeh, you do look like your mam,' he said again, in a voice of wonder.

CHAPTER 2

They made a flying start. The twins had wakened at the crack of dawn, and begun moving the camping stuff down from the attic. No sleep after that. Dad had for once got up like greased lightning, to make sure they didn't make a pig's ear of it, and Maggi had grilled everything left in the fridge. Mam hadn't liked waste. They had a slap-up breakfast, and there was still enough to pack away for emergencies. Then she'd washed up and packed the crocks in the tea-chest Dad had left in the corner.

By six, everything was stowed aboard the *QE2*, the old grey Ford Transit van with 'George R. Adams, FTC, Cabinet-maker and Builder, Roofing a Speciality' lettered on the side in Dad's careful hand. The *QE2* would hold everything, even the twins' bunk beds. You could *sleep* in the *QE2*, when she was set up for camping. You could cook in her, on the twin-burner stove. She'd been Mam's idea . . .

Dad started the engine, and let her idle to get warm, making a few curtains twitch down the terrace. The overnight rain danced on the bonnet with the vibration, and the drops ran off, or got smaller as the engine warmed up.

'A grand morning,' said Dad, drawing a deep breath. His hair was cut, and his moustache trimmed, and she'd washed his best jeans, so he looked really smart. She'd found that 'What will Ted German think?' was a powerful weapon in her hand.

And indeed it was a grand morning, with the cranes on the river faint and misty blue in the distance, and the smell of green things invading the narrow street from God knew where, as if the fields of Cheshire were coming to meet them.

There'd been a bit of a squabble about who should sit in the front with Dad, but Dad just waved the maps and the army-style route-list at the twins. 'Can you use these, then?' Baz was against anything that re-sembled a book, and Gaz was scared of making a mistake and getting told off by Dad. So there was Maggi ensconced with map, route and big thick pencil, already worrying about finding their way to the Tyne tunnel. She watched Dad check that the house's gas and water and electric were turned off for the third time, then run with the key and put it through old Mr Sanders's letter box. Then he ran back and flung himself into the driving seat as if there wasn't a moment to lose. Like he'd always done, when they went on holiday. His eyes were shining, almost as if Mam were somewhere down the road ahead, waiting for them to pick her up.

He glanced at the route-list she held.

'Sure ye can manage, hinny?'

'Aall the way to John o'Groats.' Mam's old joke. Dad's eyes grew bright, and for an awful moment she thought he was going to cry. But he just revved the engine, making a few more curtains twitch, and they were off, and the green smell was blowing in through the open window, stronger and stronger.

'Aah just hope we're doin' the right thing,' said Dad.

Maggi had no doubts. She'd have climbed Everest, if it meant leaving Doris Streeton behind.

They made good time, for the QE2. She was making a lot of noises, but they were her helpful noises, not her ominous ones. And she just managed to keep up the forty miles an hour that kept her legal on the motorway. She was fourteen years old, and although Dad was good with her, as he said, you couldn't make bricks without straw.

By nine, they were clear of Teesside, and they pulled off into a field, to give the twins a run out of the back, like they were dogs that needed an airing. After running around in circles for ten minutes, they came back and demanded a second breakfast. Maggi held out the polythene box with the nearly-cold bacon and black pudding, and they finished it between them, then ran back to the hedge to insult a herd of bullocks that had gathered with interest to receive them. Maggi made sure they had no half-bricks to hand, then sat back and let the sun warm her sandalled feet. Dad lit up (she wished he wouldn't smoke so much), drew in deep and exhaled, with his eyes half-shut.

'This is the life. Nothing like getting away from it all.'

And the ghost of Mam, sitting behind her shoulder made her say the old reply. 'It's not the gettin' away, it's the gettin' back that's the hard bit.'

He smiled lazily; it was good to see him smile like that. Then he said, 'Like to go and look over a stately home, pet?'

'Can we afford it?'

'Ted German sent me an advance. Let's have a bit o' life while we can. Might be a long time afore the next bit!'

At that point, the twins returned, as if drawn by a sixth sense, and demanded to go to York, to do the motorbike shops and amusement arcades.

But they hadn't a hope. Mam had loved a stately home. But it didn't improve the twins' temper. From the angry way cars passed them on the next bit of the journey, she knew the twins were glued to the back windows of the van, screwing up faces, putting out tongues and even two fingers at the overtaking motorists. It didn't bode well . . .

Maggi walked through the pillars and colonnades, the gilded domes and painted ceilings of the stately home in a dazed dream of glory. How did they get the cobwebs down from the high ceilings? How did they keep the black-and-white tiled floors clean? How often did they wash them? She wanted to ask the woman guide, and confide in her that she too would soon have a stately home to look after. But the woman seemed only interested in Oliver Cromwell, and the sad beheading of Charles the First, and how the King's eldest daughter died of grief afterwards.

That is, until the party were gathered closely round a great big oil-painting. The woman, in full flow about the heroic death of an eighteenth-century family mastiff, suddenly stopped, her face transfixed with horror. Maggi followed her gaze, wondering hopefully if she'd seen a ghost. But all Maggi could see, above the heads of the crowd, was the white marble head of a tall statue.

And all she could hear was a stony *tap . . . tap . . . tap . . . tap . . . tap, tap, tap, tap* which slowly died away.

But it did seem to Maggi that the white marble head had been moving; sort of swaying . . .

The colour returned to the woman's face, and she returned, stammering, to her tragic tale.

But no sooner had she resumed, than the *tap . . . tap . . . tap . . . tap . . . tap . . . tap . . . tap* started again. And again it seemed to Maggi that the statue moved. She wondered if it was some interesting feature of the house that the guide would speak about next.

The sorely-tried woman returned to her tale a second time, only now she was talking about the 'mamily fastiff'.

Tap . . . tap . . . tap . . . tap . . . tap . . . tap.

Then Dad seemed to go berserk. He plunged through the crowd with a great inarticulate cry. The people parted like the Red Sea in amazement. Revealing Dad standing at the base of the statue, with each muscular hand gripping the denim collar of one of the twins.

'You pair of little . . .'

Please, prayed Maggi, please God, *don't* let him say it in public. He's not in the army now.

Dad went no further. Either it was an answer to her prayer, or Dad couldn't think of a word bad enough. Then he yelled, 'You were rocking that statue, the pair of you. Weren't you?'

'Only a bit,' choked Gaz.

'Only a bit o' fun,' choked Baz.

'The man who carved that statue, *hundreds* of years ago, spent half his life carving it. And all you can think of to do . . . you're not *mine* – Aah'll swear Aah nivvor fathered ye . . . aargh!' And in a second, Dad had picked up a struggling twin under each arm, and was bearing them off towards the door, their wildly kicking feet a threat to more than one masterpiece.

At the open door, Dad gave one gigantic heave, and the twins were sprawling on the gravel outside.

'And you'll *stay* there,' roared Dad, 'till ye're fit to mix wi' decent people.' The twins got up and glared at him, rubbing various parts of their anatomy, and looking like they didn't know what had hit them. At that point, Dad seemed to relent. He reached in his pocket and threw a coin that glinted in the air at Gaz's midriff. Gaz, in spite of his bewilderment, caught it. After all, it was money. Then Dad finished, 'Go and find the shop and buy yourself Mars Bars an' go an' sit in the middle o' that lawn, where Aah can keep me eye on you an' don't you dare move a muscle.'

The twins gaped at him open-mouthed. When he rejoined the tour party, the party gaped open-mouthed. But there had been a murmur of approval, and one woman had said, 'Our Jack could do wi' a bit o' that, Tom!'

'Right, missus,' said Dad to the guide. 'Fire away. You were talkin' about this poor mongrel dog here . . .'

* * *

Afterwards, Gaz crept up to Maggi, and said in an awed tone, 'What's got into me dad?'

'What's got into him is what's going to stay in him from now on,' said Maggi sharply. 'Our dad's changed, and the sooner you believe that, the better for you.' Gaz moved away thoughtfully. He would talk to Baz about it. Gaz was the one you could get to listen, if you got him on his own. And he was the only one Baz ever listened to.

They got to Northwich about quarter to five, which was later than Dad wanted, because the *QE2* had died twice coming over the Pennines. Dad had desperately given her the kiss of life on the hard shoulder before they got towed away, which would have cost fifty pounds they hadn't got.

They had a desperate scramble to find the house agents, before they shut. Maggi gazed through the window of E. N. Morris, Estate Agents, Auctioneers and Valuers. There was a lady sitting at a desk typing, as pretty as a picture, and just as thoroughly painted, though she looked untouched by human hand. Her long legs were superbly crossed, and her long finger-nails pecked at the typewriter with disdain, as if it was a dead cat. Maggi had no wish to be despised by her.

'Come in wi' me, pet,' said Dad. 'Ye might as well see the action – y're doin' half the work.' She thought Dad wasn't looking forward much to being despised

22

by the lady either. He went in with a rush, all shoulders, like he was looking for a fight.

'Me name's Adams. Come for the keys of the Abbey. It's Mr Morris I want.'

'Which Mr Morris, *sir*? We have three Mr Morrises!'

It was obviously the lady's favourite joke. She said 'sir' nastily, like a dog snarling.

'Any Mr Morris ye've got lyin' aboot handy, hinny!'

The lady flared her delicious nostrils, obviously thinking that being called 'hinny' was tantamount to rape.

'One that knaas aboot the keys, eh? That's a good lass!' Dad was doing his broad accent on purpose. He always did when anybody tried coming posh.

The lady shuddered delicately, and pressed a silver button on a black box.

'There's a *gentleman* called Adams to see you, Mr Morris.'

'There's a canny lass,' said Dad. 'Aah knew ye could manage, if ye tried.'

Mr Morris was a large man, with blond hair going silver, and ruddy cheeks like a farmer. Only his blue eyes were small and sharp and mean, and a little smile played constantly round his face, as if everything was a joke that only he was clever enough to see.

'The Abbey keys, eh?' Eyebrow cocked; little smile. Dad said nowt. 'Mouldering old heap – full of dry rot.

Victorian architecture at its worst. Should've been pulled down years ago. Nice park. Take a nice little estate of executive bungalows. Planners won't give us permission; yet.'

Maggi's heart sank; all her dreams ran out of her, like water out of a leaky hot-water bottle. Then she realized with horror that Mr Morris was enjoying, with a little smile, the misery on her face.

'Qualified man, are you, Mr Adams? Qualified to be a site foreman?'

'FTC,' said Dad. He spat it out like it was the rudest words he knew.

Little smile. 'I only asked,' said Mr Morris, 'because I could use a good site foreman. We've got a nice little estate going up at Brunner Park. Four-bedroomed executive detached . . . hundred thousand a time.'

'Aah'm workin' for Ted German,' said Dad.

'Oh, the Marigold *Trust*. They're poor as church mice. Not a penny to their name . . .'

Maggi desperately tried to keep the misery out of her face, so that Mr Morris's little eyes and smiling pink mouth couldn't feed on it.

'Aah came for the keys,' said Dad.

'Ah, yes, the *keys*,' said Mr Morris, closing his eyes and savouring the joke, as if it was a pint of his favourite beer. 'Ninety-eight keys, none of them labelled. Ninety-eight keys, and they say there are ninety-nine rooms . . . what will you find in the ninety-ninth room, I wonder? Perhaps the ghost of the good *nun*?'

'Ghosts?' gasped Maggi, knowing her eyes had grown bigger than saucers.

'Oh, those old monks were nasty people,' said Mr Morris cheerfully. 'Well-hated locally. They squeezed the poor till their pips squeaked, to build their great big church. The locals murdered one, and cut off his head and played football with it . . .'

'I'll have the keys *now*, Mr Morris,' said Dad, sounding angrier than Maggi had ever heard him.

'There's a stupid Victorian novel in the public library, all about it,' said Mr Morris, not moving an inch. 'They say the nun was in love with the last abbot, and he got her in the family way and gave her the sailor's farewell, so she hanged herself . . .'

'Go and wait in the van, Maggi,' said Dad. She hoped he wasn't going to hit Mr Morris . . .

'And here's the keys,' said Mr Morris, producing a huge rusting bunch, nearly as big as a football. 'A Miss MacFarlane left them for you – some doddering old spinster – secretary of the Marigold Trust . . .'

Dad grabbed them like he wished they were Mr Morris's throat.

'Just a friendly warning,' said Mr Morris. 'That Abbey has broken a lot of hearts. They tried to make it into a country club, and it went bankrupt. They tried a school of accountants, a civil defence centre, a school. All . . . *pffft.*' He drew his hand sharply across his throat. 'When it's broken *your* heart, Mr Adams, come back and build bungalows for me . . . I do need a sound man.'

'Me heart doesn't break that easy,' said Dad.

'I'll be waiting,' said Mr Morris.

'I'd sooner shovel pig-manure,' said Dad.

Just for a second, the little smile faltered. Then it was back again, as Mr Morris leaned back in his chair. His eyes vanished into a network of little creases of pleasure. He waved a plump pink hand, in farewell or dismissal.

When they got back to the QE2, the twins had started a sit-in, on the running-board. They sat there and glowered, with their elbows on their knees and their chins on their fists. They had suffered great unfairness, declared Gaz, who was always the spokesman. They had been cooped up in the back all day. They had not seen a motorbike shop or an amusement arcade for forty-eight hours and they would assuredly die of deprivation. Dad, having been tough with them once today, got a fit of conscience. He let them trail the family all over the town. They found two bike shops, (shut, thank God – they were terrors once they got inside, fingering the gloves and helmets) and one amusement arcade, unfortunately still open. Not until they'd spent every penny of their holiday money, and borrowed next week's pocket money, and begun kicking the machines did they let themselves be led away. And then only on condition that they were fed . . .

Luckily, the Seafarer was still open. They demolished mounds of fish and chips, and scrounged more chips off Dad and Maggi, reaching their grubby little hands across the red plastic like predatory crabs. And demanded bread and butter and apple turnovers to follow. But then their eyes sort of glazed over, and Maggi knew they wouldn't be any bother at all for two whole hours. And there were only six miles to go to the Abbey.

With two miles to go, at nine o'clock precisely, the *QE2* went on strike. Three hours later, Maggi was still sitting on an old milestone, half-buried in long grass, that read CHESTER 14 MILES. It was a lovely warm evening, and the smells of the Cheshire night, grass and trees and cow-manure and some flower, unknown in the dark, filled her nostrils. But you could get too much even of the smells of a Cheshire night.

The others were huddled over the bonnet of the van.

'For God's sake hold that torch steady, Gaz,' said Dad, his voice sharp with anger. 'And where's that three-eighths monkey-wrench? If you divven't fettle-up, we'll be here aall neet.'

Half an hour later, they reached the gate of the Abbey. Only there wasn't a gate, just two sandstone walls curving inwards, and a big signboard saying:

FOXWIST ABBEY

THE MARIGOLD TRUST

ADMITTANCE ON BUSINESS ONLY

The sign was new, but even in the light of the head-lights you could see people had been throwing bricks at it; one side was splitting. Dad made a noise of disgust, deep in his throat. He made more as they drove up the drive. The drive had once been tarmacked, but it was now full of potholes that made the *QE2* lurch and sway as in a heavy sea. In the head-lights the potholes looked as big and deep as the craters of the moon. On each side unrolled a great avenue of old beech trees. But every second tree seemed to have fallen; the great trunks lay branchless, like dead men who had lost their arms.

'By gum,' said Dad, 'folk mustn't go short o' logs round here.'

And every so often, under the still-standing beeches, there were cars parked. Maggi thought they were empty at first, till a timid pale female face raised itself and peered through a windscreen at their headlights, only to vanish abruptly, as if pulled down by somebody else inside.

'Who *are* they, Dad?'

'Poachers, Aah expect,' said Dad stiffly, from deep in his throat.

The drive went on and on and on. Later, they were to joke that the gate was nearer to Northwich than to the Abbey. But that night, all Maggi could think about was how far the Abbey was from anywhere . . .

Then suddenly, they were there. There was an entrance gate to the forecourt, with pillars on each side, surmounted by great stone dragons holding shields with coats of arms in front of them. But the gates were fastened together with a rusty chain and padlock. Wheel-ruts led through a gap smashed in the wall, twenty yards further on. The forecourt had once been gravelled; but now the gravel was slashed with deep ruts, and low islands of mud had pushed their way through, on which grew jungles of tall scraggy-looking weeds. There was a roughly lettered sign saying: WARNING – GUARD DOGS but it was leaning over badly, and people had been throwing mud and bricks at that as well.

'No point to warning guard dogs,' said Dad. 'Guard dogs can't read.'

But nobody laughed.

The Abbey was a low, long L-shape. The front was a dull grey stone, and the side bit was brick. At the joint of the L was a huge clock tower, sixty feet high, with a pointed roof. One clockface said ten to four, and the other half past ten.

'Aah musta taken the wrong turn,' said Dad. 'We're in London an' they've sent Big Ben to welcome us.'

Again, nobody laughed.

There were lots of tall black chimneys, sticking up through the roof all over the place. But the thing that struck Maggi was the long rows of pointed windows, small on the ground floor, but huge on the floor above. There was a moon out now, and clouds were being driven across it by the warm wind. The wind-blown moonlit clouds were reflected in the great windows, so the place seemed lit up within by a ghostly blue light, and in the swirling, Maggi kept on thinking she saw faces looking down on them . . .

'Well, sittin' here won't buy the bairn a new shirt,' said Dad, and heaved himself out of the cab with a pretty discouraged sigh.

Even the twins, sleepy now, were quiet and still, with nothing to say.

'Drat it,' said Dad. 'This key fits – but it won't turn.'

They had pressed the three different bell-buttons,

and pulled a handle, but no sound emerged. Maggi had never expected one to – everything grated under her hand with rust. Dad had undone the bunch of keys, and now had them in two heaps, tried and untried. The twins had gone back to the van, to try and have a kip, they said.

Maggi stared at the great pointed door, with its rusty curling hinges. It looked like a church door – but bleached and dead, with grass growing against it, like a church door the vicar never used.

'Perhaps there's another door, Dad?'

'Aah'll go on trying this so-and-so. It *should* open.' He turned the curly handle dreamily, lost in the mechanics of the lock; far more interested in getting it to turn than in getting into the house.

'Shall I go and look for another door, Dad?'

He considered; she knew he was thinking about the danger of strange men, prowlers. But who would be out here, miles from anywhere, at one o'clock in the morning?

She ran off for the corner, before he could say no.

'Tek care!' he shouted after her.

She came to a hedge so high it seemed to block out the sky. A flight of white steps ran down through it, white in the moonlight.

And there was a man. A huge naked man, standing on top of a block of stone, waiting to jump down on her. For a second her heart tried to squeeze up through her mouth. But he was so still, so pure white in the moonlight. And his nose was worn away by rain, and his eyes just dead drilled holes. And dark moss grew up his strong legs, like some awful disease. But he had *everything*. She tiptoed past, trying not to look at him . . . but looking just the same.

There was a whole row of them; men and ladies alternately, all down the long brick side of the house. They watched her as she went, with their blind drilled holes of eyes. And behind them, the windows of the house watched her too. And for the first time she realized how big this house was. What a long walk round it was going to be, before she got back to Dad. But she wasn't turning back; she'd rather die than face the jeering of Baz and Gaz.

As she approached the next corner, she saw that the shadow of the house lay across the garden like a black sword. On the side of the house furthest from Dad she would have to walk in total darkness. And if she screamed for help, he wouldn't even hear her.

Now or never. She plunged through another great hedge; down another flight of steps – and stopped. She could see nothing but the great black bulk of the house against the dim moonglare. But there was a smell, an utterly heavenly smell – she groped forward. Something thin and sharp grabbed at her T-shirt, catching her back. But she didn't scream, because she knew it wasn't a hand. No, this thing was thin and stiff and – ouch, prickly. As she struggled to disentangle it from her shoulder, something soft and cold touched her cheek and the heavenly smell became quite overpowering. She grabbed for the cold soft thing; it felt like a small loose cabbage; then it fell apart in her hand, leaving a handful of petals. She was in a rose garden. She pressed the handful of petals into her face and breathed deep. And for the first time she knew the house loved her, had given her a marvellous present.

She could see a little better now. Dim gravel paths among the huge overgrown rose bushes. She wandered from rose to rose, having a good smell of each. She felt she was in Paradise, with only the sound of her own two feet walking.

No, there was another noise; another scrunching behind the scrunching of her own feet walking. Her feet stopped. The other scrunching continued.

Something was eating. Something was being eaten . . .

She remembered a film on the telly. A furry beastly face against a background of roses – *Beauty and the Beast*. The awful Beast had lived in a rose garden . . .

The scrunching was ahead of her. She must go back. She began to back away.

But there was scrunching behind her, too. More than one of them ... eating. She stopped, utterly paralysed.

The thing eating in front came nearer. Scrunch, scrunch, scrunch. Then the silence. Then feet, hard bony feet, tiptoeing towards her.

Then scrunch, scrunch, scrunch, just above her head.

She had to look up. She saw the face. A long white face, with a straggle of white beard, that waggled as the jaws scrunched. A long bony white nose. Mad oblong yellow eyes. And ... little horns curving from the forehead.

She felt distantly her lungs gathering air for the biggest scream in the world. Then the creature spoke.

'Baa-aaah,' it said.

And terror collapsed into the shape of a white goat, standing on its hind legs to eat the roses.

She ran back all the way. It seemed to her dreadful that goats were eating the beautiful roses. When she reached the front, the great door was open, and light was streaming across the rutted gravel. Dad was standing with his hands on his hips, looking content.

She was so breathless she was a long time making him understand she hadn't been attacked. But he did *understand* about the roses; he understood it was *important*, even in the middle of the night, after a whole day driving.

'By, come on, lads! We can't have next door's goats eatin' our roses!' She ran back with him, loving him so much she felt her heart would burst. The twins, with the promise of attacking something, regained all their lost energy and ran ahead whooping. The goats never stood a chance; though one of them tried a bit of butting, they were whacked from the rose garden with sticks that miraculously appeared from nowhere in the twins' hands. Dad forced closed the rusty gates of the garden, while the twins pursued the beaten foe with ghastly screams.

'They went through a hole in the hedge,' said Gaz. 'Reckon they won't be back in a hurry.'

They closed the creaking door behind them, and journeyed into the great house, working from light-switch to light-switch like African explorers working their way through a stone jungle.

They were in a corridor so long that the far end seemed to vanish into a smoky mist. Rows of pillars on either side, and a vaulted roof overhead. It was all painted a shocking orange, like an ice lolly or something in a funfair. But that only made it more ghostly. In one wall there were windows you couldn't look out of, because they were full of coloured scenes and figures. Men in flowing robes and turbans and beards pointed at walled cities that fell down as they were pointed at. Cringing naked men were thrown by devils down the throats of great dragons . . . Maggi eyed each one fearfully, as if they were a timetable of doom.

'S'only stuff out of the Bible,' said Dad. 'Nothin' to worry about.'

So why was he whispering? Why were the twins totally silent, and even walking on tiptoe? As they passed one iron-studded door, Gaz muttered, 'Knock twice an' ask for Dracula!'

Baz snickered, suddenly and explosively. But it only made the silence nastier afterwards.

They came to a notice board, with yellowing sheets of paper pinned on with rusty drawing pins. Red marks of damp streamed down from the drawing pins. It was a notice giving end-of-term arrangements for the Welwyn School of Accountancy. The date was Christmas 1975.

At the end of the corridor, a staircase ascended. Another dragon with a coat of arms sat on the newel post, but this time carved in shiny, dark, dusty wood, and with a beak so curved and sharp he looked as if he might bite if you got close enough. At the top, Dad tried doors. The first three wouldn't open; the fourth gave onto a kitchen. Dozens of black beetles ran for cover across the bare boarded floor, as Dad flicked the light on. But there was a kettle on a stove, with cold water in it. And a mug and plate washed up in the drying-rack, and a copy of the *Guardian* on the table from three days ago.

'Civilization,' said Dad. 'That Miss MacFarlane musta left it – that old lady who's the secretary. See if you can find some tea bags, our Maggi – Aah could do wi' a brew.'

At that moment, all the lights went out. In the total blackness, Maggi could hear Dad clicking the light-switch off and on. But it was useless. Because Maggi could see through the open door that the staircase lights were off as well; and the ones they'd left on in the long corridor downstairs. All dark; they might as well be in the middle of the Great Pyramid of Egypt.

Somewhere in the dark, the fuses must have gone.

She was just on the point of bursting into a scream, when Dad said calmly, 'Where's me torch? The lads'll have to kip down in the van for the night. You an' me can get our sleepin' bags an' kip down here, Maggi.'

CHAPTER 3

She wakened suddenly in blackness, knowing only she was in a huge icy-cold space. Then she saw the shape of the great pointed window, dark blue against the blackness, and thought she'd got herself locked inside a church.

But her exploring fingers brought reassurance. She was on a blow-up camping mattress on the floor. In a sleeping bag – the one Dad usually used. The smell of him, putty, paint and fag-smoke, comforted her a bit.

But Dad should be with her in the kitchen. She held her breath, but she couldn't hear him breathing. Had he gone off and left her? Died in the night, like Mam?

Her hand, like a poor cold crawling spider, crept across the dusty floor. A candlestick moved to her touch, with a small hollow 'boing'. A matchbox rattled drily, and seemed to dodge away from the tips of her fingers in the dark. But she pursued and trapped it. The first match snapped off at the head, and leapt away like a small bright comet. With the second, held in shaking fingers, she lit the wobbly bedribbled candle. Its light spread out with agonizing slowness. Then she saw Dad in his sleeping bag, on

38

the floor by the sink unit. Just a tuft of blond hair showing, and a hand that clenched the sleeping bag tight enough to throttle it. She stared, waiting for the sleeping bag to rise and fall, to tell her he was alive. Instead, he turned over, groaned to himself and mumbled something about 'two-by-fours'.

She lay back with a deep sigh of relief, staring at the dim faraway ceiling. It was all right.

Then, suddenly, the need to go to the loo stabbed her like a merciless dagger. Oh, *no*! She should have gone before she went to bed! But she *had* gone before she went to bed. It was this terrible cold that was doing it. She looked round, desperately, for any means to make the journey unnecessary. But Dad was in the way of everything. She had to go out of this door and turn right. Then first left and second right. Dad had drummed it into her. But it had been spooky enough with Dad and his torch. Now she only had a candle that could be blown out by the merest puff of draught. She'd have to wake Dad . . . ask where he'd put the torch.

But he groaned again in his sleep, ever so weary, and she hadn't the heart.

She'd been sleeping in her jeans. She slipped her anorak on and put the hood up against the unbelievable cold. She groped for her sandals, but the merciless dagger struck her again; it would not stab many more times before it shamed her. She left the sandals.

The stone flags of the corridor bit at her feet, cold as tomb stones, but she was on her way. Turn right . . . first left . . . second right . . .

There was a tiny light ahead of her, bobbing like her own candle-flame. With a dark shape behind it, and a white blur that might be a face above. She stopped: the other light stopped. Her flame lengthened in the stillness; the other flame lengthened too.

She laughed shakily to herself. There must be a great dusty mirror at the end of this corridor, that they hadn't noticed in the dark, before. Fancy being about to scream at her own stupid reflection!

Except . . . the dark shape behind the flame in the mirror seemed much bigger than her; the pale blur of the face much higher up. Was it a trick mirror that made you look tall, like they had in fairgrounds?

Another stab below warned her to get on. But, as she raised a foot, the figure in the mirror seemed to move towards her. She put her own foot back abruptly. But the figure in the mirror kept on moving towards her. Got bigger and bigger. Far taller than she was. She could see long pale fingers now, cupped round the flame. And the face had a dark cowl round it, and a touch of white at the throat that had nothing to do with her own red T-shirt. And it was draped to its feet in black, with just a flicker where the feet were moving. And the face was a woman's face, with long thin nose and pursed lips and huge dark eyes . . .

She wanted to run; but her feet seemed frozen to the flags. She wanted to shout for Dad, but her throat seemed full of sticky cobwebs, and she knew he would never hear her round all those twists of corridor. She wished she could *faint*, before the ghost of the nun covered her in the cold of the grave.

'Who on earth are *you*?' snapped the ghost, cross as a schoolteacher. 'Standing there like a little spook? You nearly frightened the life out of me.' Then the nun burst out laughing, though it was pretty shaky laughter, and in an instant turned into a very tall lady with an anorak hood pulled up over her ears, and clutching a long grey blanket over a frilly lace nightdress.

'Maggi Adams,' Maggi said stoutly. 'And if I don't get to the loo in a minute—'

'Two minds and a single thought,' said the lady. 'You go first; I can hang on. Only don't pull the chain unless you have to; it takes ages to refill.'

Afterwards, Maggi felt better, but she was shivering uncontrollably.

'Better come to my room,' said the lady. 'I've got a thermos full of soup, in case I wake up in the middle of the night.'

'Do you sleep here, all *alone*?'

'Of course. I'm in charge. I'm the secretary of the Marigold Trust.'

'Aren't you scared of ghosts?'

'If there are any ghosts, I'm sure they wish me well in my efforts to bring this house back to life.' The lady said it with a rush, like someone swatting at a fly. Like she didn't want the idea of ghosts in her mind. But she must be terribly brave . . . Maggi wouldn't do it for a million pounds.

'The lights seemed to have failed again,' said the lady calmly, handing her a cup of steaming soup.

'They went as we came in. My dad'll fix them in the morning.'

'Oh, *Adams*. Mr *Adams*,' said the lady. 'I was expecting you, only when you didn't turn up by midnight I went to bed.'

Maggi stared round the room. It was a lot warmer and more cheerful than the kitchen. There was a dim orange glow in the grate, and the wide hearth was full of old sawn logs, boxes of chopped sticks, buckets of coal, newspaper and what looked like a lemonade bottle full of paraffin.

'I've been rather camping out while I've been on my own, I'm afraid,' said the lady. 'I'm used to roughing it. Not as bad as VSO in Jamaica *I* can tell you. If they don't like you there, they start nailing dead birds to

42

your front door, and then it's time to come home *quick* . . .' She laughed gaily at the memory; then stopped rather abruptly. 'Anyway, we'll soon have a good blaze going.'

'Are you a teacher?' asked Maggi.

'Does it show that much?'

'Well, you're quite good at pretending to be cheerful, even when you don't feel it. That's like teachers.'

'Touché.'

'Yewhat?' asked Maggi, a bit rudely she thought. But then saying things you couldn't understand was a bit like teachers too.

The fire soon blazed up; casting jumping shadows around the walls. The room was a bit like the lady – a lot of cheerful, interesting things trying to cover up a lot of gloom. There were slightly tattered posters covering the grim grey walls. One of a Spanish bull-fight, next to a splattered one saying 'Stop the bloody whaling'. Why did the lady want to save whales but not bulls? There was a poster of the wine-growing districts of France, and one of that fairy-tale castle in Bavaria, and one of Elton John in his straw hat.

There was a jam jar of wild flowers, rather droop-ing, on the mantelpiece, a guitar propped up in the corner, a blue sleeping bag in the middle of a four-poster bed, and a huge blue rucksack nearby. And a table with three-and-a-half legs and a portable type-writer on top.

But although the fire gave great light, it didn't give all that much heat. Maggi clutched the steaming soup with both hands, gratefully, but she couldn't stop shivering. The lady noticed and pulled a big tartan rug off the bed, and tucked it round Maggi with gentle hands. 'Can't have you going down with pneumonia, can we?'

'Thank you, Miss MacFarlane—'

'Not Miss MacFarlane, *Ms* MacFarlane.' She drew out the *Ms*, making it sound like a bee buzzing. 'Mzzzzzz MacFarlane. Why should I have to tell every Tom, Dick and Harry that I'm not married? Mzzzzzzzz.' Then she flew on with her fascinating account of life in Jamaica, as if the interruption had never happened.

Maggi began to get really warm. She was sitting in a big old armchair covered with worn velvet, and although there was a loose spring sticking into her bottom, it was a very cosy enfolding kind of chair. Ms MacFarlane had a lovely voice, like a TV news-reader's, only even posher. So soothing. Maggi wanted to go on listening about the endless wonders of Jamaica, but she was so sleepy. She thought dreamily that Mzz MacFarlane was like a great dam, full of talk, and that she, Maggi, had made a hole in the dam, and that the ideas would flow all night, and all to-morrow and . . . she wondered how long it was since Mzz MacFarlane had had anyone to talk to . . .

Her eyes closed. She thought she must get back to the kitchen, or Dad would wake up and find her gone and have a fit. But it was so *warm* here . . . Mzz MacFarlane's voice swept over her like the waves of the sea, and then the waves grew very distant.

The last thing she remembered was gentle hands tucking her in. Just like Mam's. It was funny, after so long . . .

Maggi slept.

CHAPTER 4

S he was awakened by the sun streaming in at the uncurtained windows. She felt scrumpled and dirty from sleeping in her clothes, her bottom was almost numb where the chair-spring had battered it all night, and she had a crick in her neck. The roaring fire had become a bed of grey ash, the walls were cracked and peeling, and damp in one corner, and the whole place looked like the worst kind of second-hand shop.

Mzz MacFarlane slept on, one bare arm outside the sleeping bag. She slept gracefully, with her mouth shut, not snoring.

She was not, of course, old. Not as old as nasty Mr Morris had said, anyway. Not as old as Dad, Maggi reckoned. There weren't any deep lines on her forehead or mouth. She wasn't pretty; too bony to be pretty. But if she'd been a feller, you would've called her handsome, with her long pale straight nose and tall forehead, and a pretty determined chin. Her red eyebrows curved clear and clean, and they hadn't been mucked about with. There was no trace of lipstick. Maggi knew somehow that she didn't use make-up. There was a comb on the bedside table, and a little pair of scissors, and soap and flannel, and a tooth-brush and toothpaste. But no make-up. Her visible arm was long and white and graceful; her hand had beautiful long fingers, but the nails were cut short, and not painted.

She looked sad, asleep. Just like Dad. (Maggi wondered if all adults looked sad, asleep.) She looked like the Sleeping Beauty in a junk shop. Only more like the Prince than the Sleeping Beauty. Then she murmured and half turned in her sleep; Maggi blushed at her rudeness in staring, and fled.

Instinct would have driven her towards the kitchen, even if Dad hadn't been there. She felt better in kitchens. She liked the kitchen at home better than any other room in the house, because in the kitchen everything was where *she* said; everybody did what *she* said.

But Dad had gone; his sleeping bag and hers were rolled up neatly in one corner. And this kitchen was huge, and dark. Some windows were broken and blocked up with bits of old cardboard.

The lights still didn't work; the floor was filthy with mud. Maggi went round in a fury, opening cupboards and drawers and finding weird things. Instead of corn-flakes there was a polythene bag full of oats and nuts that looked revolting. The fridge seemed to be work-ing (though the light didn't go on) but it was only full of tubs of queer-smelling yoghurt, and plastic boxes full of strange green leaves. She tried the electric cooker without hope, and could have wept for joy when one of the rings (not the one she'd expected) slowly glowed cherry-red. It was like finding a friend. She filled the kettle (a whistling kettle of a strange mauve colour with the whistle missing). Dad would need his early morning brew. She rummaged around and assembled two cups without saucers, a mug and a glass. There was a half-pint of milk, which should've been kept in the fridge. It was all bleary and stuck to the sides, but didn't smell too bad. She threw dying wild flowers out of a lidless teapot. There was a tin of ancient tea leaves.

She brewed up in triumph. Then couldn't find any sugar . . .

Then there was a great and thunderous knocking on the distant front door; loud enough to wake the whole of Cheshire. The twins were awake and ravening, like wild beasts. If they weren't fed quick, things would start getting broken. And she had nothing to give them, not even toast. There was a sort of loaf, but it was dark and hard and full of whole lumps of grain. And a weird melting soya-oil marge. They'd never eat *that*.

She trailed down to let them in, feeling like an Early Christian about to be martyred. They waltzed round the kitchen, bright as pitiless buttons, opening all the drawers and cupboards and saying things like, 'I wouldn't give that to a *pig*,' and, 'They must keep rabbits,' and 'Eurk.' Tears were gathering in the corners of her eyes when Dad appeared, looking as black and filthy as a sweep, in his best jeans, but remarkably cheerful.

'Amazing house this, pet. I've just been up inspecting the roof . . . Is breakfast ready? Aah cud eat a horse.'

'There's *nothing*,' she screamed at him. 'Just stupid oats and health shop muck. That woman must be *mad*!'

'Good morning,' said Mzz MacFarlane, appearing in the door just in time to hear, wearing a livid green tracksuit with 'Buenos Aires' spelt out vertically down the trousers in orange. Her hair stood up like she'd been pulled through a bush backwards.

The twins began to giggle at the sight of her.

'Out,' roared Dad, grabbing the twins by the scruff of their necks, and again throwing them out bodily.

'Everybody into the *QE2*. We'll have breakfast in Northwich. Make a list, Maggi, all you need to cook.' Then he turned to Mzz MacFarlane. 'Good morning, madam. We'll leave you to get your breakfast in peace, instead of pieces.'

Maggi was proud of him.

* * *

By lunch time, Maggi was starting to feel sane again. Dad had worked wonders. He'd got the lights back on. He found a spare bulb for the fridge in his tool-kit in the van. By twelve, the twins' bunk beds were out of the van and assembled in the room next to the kitchen. By half-past she had her own room, with a long couch he'd dragged in from somewhere. It was comfy to lie on, even if it was decorated with battered golden cherubs and bunches of leaves, and felt damp if she lay on it for more than a minute.

Dad knocked her a few nails in the door, to hang her clothes on. Even found her a bit of hearthrug and a rusty one-bar electric fire that worked. She left it on to air the couch. She felt better, having her own private lair with her books, and worked like a Trojan in the kitchen. Dad had given her two pounds of bribe-money for the twins, and she worked them like Trojans' slaves, washing down everything with hot water from her own electric kettle from home. By one o'clock, all the new groceries were in newly washed cupboards; all her pots and pans and crocks were arrayed on the newly washed shelves; the floor, washed free of its coating of mud, revealed a very decent set of red and black vinyl tiles; and she felt ready to face the world. Dad had made shades for the naked bulbs out of white cardboard, scrounged from goodness knows where; Mzz MacFarlane lent her more tattered posters to cover up the holes in the plaster, and it was a kitchen she could have faced her Aunt Maureen in.

By the time the twins thought about screaming for lunch, she had toast done and baked beans on the stove. They had them in front of them within two minutes; that stopped their silly mouths.

Mzz MacFarlane accepted a cup of tea, though she refused sugar and dropped in little white tablets from a plastic box with a button on top.

'Them's speed-pills,' muttered Baz to Gaz, in a whisper everyone could hear. 'Purple hearts. She's a druggie!'

But Mzz MacFarlane was too busy rummaging in the fridge for the funny green leaves and rock-hard bread to notice.

'No – she's a horse,' said Baz. 'Only horses eat green leaves.'

'She can't be a horse and on dope,' objected Gaz, reasonably enough.

'Course she can – they dope horses to win the Derby . . .'

'If certain persons don't shut up,' said Dad, 'certain persons could lose a week's pocket money.'

Baz and Gaz removed the last beans from their plates with the avidity of locusts, and vanished. Dad followed soon after. Maggi could tell he couldn't really cope with Mzz MacFarlane. Mzz MacFarlane didn't know how to cope with Dad, either. Sometimes she addressed him as if she was the Lady of the House, and sometimes she tried to be matey. Every time she spoke it was different. Maggi thought Dad didn't mind her being the Great Lady; it was the matiness he couldn't take. Maggi could tell he thought it was as real as a three-pound note.

Maggi finished, and began to clear up. Mzz MacFarlane went on sitting, staring out of the window and tapping her elegant white fingers on the table.

'Could I have your plate, please?' asked Maggi timidly. 'To wash up?'

'I'll give you a hand,' said Mzz MacFarlane. But she went on sitting, tapping her finger, even when Maggi had the crocks washed and nicely stacked.

Maggi started to dry up. The tea towel was new, bought in Northwich market and rather hard to use.

'You're quite the little housewife,' said Mzz MacFarlane, too bright and rather patronizing, like a teacher trying to be chummy.

'Nobody else to do it,' said Maggi abruptly.

'Do you cook and . . . everything?'

'Yeah.' Maggi thought that if Mzz MacFarlane said it was terrible for a child of her age to have to do all that, she'd scream. All the women said that. Especially Doreen Streeton . . .

But Mzz MacFarlane only said rather sadly, 'I'm hopeless at cooking. Nobody ever taught me.'

'Didn't yer mam . . . ?'

'I was sent away to school. My parents were abroad all the time.'

No mam. No dad either. How awful.

'Couldn't yer mam teach you now?'

'Both my parents are dead . . .'

No mam, no dad. Ever. Maggi closed her eyes in horror. No wonder Mzz MacFarlane looked so sad in her sleep . . .

'Would you like to eat with us tonight?'

'What are you having?'

'Only bacon and eggs. With tinned rhubarb and custard. But you're welcome!' Maggi suddenly thought Mzz MacFarlane was too thin. Mam would've said she needed fattening up a bit.

'I never think about what I eat,' said Mzz MacFarlane. 'I'm usually too busy thinking about other things.'

'Bacon an' egg won't do you any harm.'

'Doesn't it worry you about factory-farming – the way they keep the pigs and chickens?'

'Never think about it,' said Maggi stoutly (though she did), 'I'm just glad we've got the money to buy food. You gotta eat something. But you can have baked beans an' chips if you'd rather . . . I've got half a tin of beans over.'

Funny, now she was talking like the mam, and Mzz MacFarlane like the kid.

Mzz MacFarlane sighed and came to a big decision. 'Thank you very much . . . it seems wrong not to eat with everyone else.'

'I'll cook for five in future, then!'

'I'd better do that drying up.'

'It's done,' said Maggi. 'Besides, the twins do the washing up. It's what they get their pocket money for. Give the little beggars an inch, they'll take a mile.'

'I must do something. I can't let you do it all. I'll take the washing to the launderette.'

Maggi gaped in horror. There were holes in most of Dad's socks. Darned, but still holes. And the twins' underpants and vests were raggy . . .

It seemed to occur to Mzz MacFarlane that she'd gone too far.

'Well, I'll drive you to the launderette, then. I'll do mine, you do yours!'

Suddenly, they smiled at each other; and they were real smiles.

CHAPTER 5

After lunch next day, Maggi finished scraping the new potatoes and stood them on the drainer in the big old earthenware bowl she'd found in a cupboard. Mr German had said the bowl was antique, Victorian. Mr German said the cupboard was antique, Victorian. It pleased Maggi, using things the Victorian cook had used. She imagined that cook, big and plump and full of importance, bustling about and giving orders to dozens of kitchen maids.

She glanced round the kitchen. It was all square, spotless. Now the Victorian cook would have put her feet up, until it was time to lay the tray for afternoon tea. But Maggi couldn't have felt less like putting her feet up. The huge bunch of ninety-eight keys tugged again at the corner of her eye, from where they hung on the Welsh dresser; they'd been tugging at her eye ever since breakfast; tempting her like some dark delicious sin, making her insides feel quite hollow. And the whole house was tempting her now, because she knew she was quite alone in it. The twins were playing footie in the meadow beyond the rose garden. The black-and-white ball rose, slow as a moon at that distance. Their endlessly squabbling voices came faint as the birds in the woods.

Dad, Mzz MacFarlane and Mr German were standing together in the middle of the rose garden. Mr German was talking loudly (did he ever stop?) and waving his arms about, pointing at something on the roof above the kitchen windows, and making vertical and horizontal chopping movements with his hands. Dad said all architects did that. Mr German was a funny-looking man, sort of antique, Victorian, with his balding head like an egg, and sidewhiskers down the sides of his face, and his striped shirt with a plain white collar. He was actually so proud of his yellow braces with patterns on them he kept showing them off by sticking his thumbs in them.

Mzz MacFarlane was quite silent for once, staring at Mr German in admiration and listening to his every word. Maybe she was in love with him?

Maggi wished her the best of British luck, in a distant, sunny-afternoon sort of way. She had her own fish to fry; she lifted down the keys with a grunt of effort.

Under the impact of the afternoon sun the house looked quite different. The sun's rays streamed in through the huge pointed windows like searchlights, in which dustmotes rose and fell like midges. The sunbeams hit the dusty oak boards of the old floors, making pools of molten, trellised gold, from which the light bounced upwards again, making diamond trellis-patterns on the grey plaster ceiling. And then bounced down again, onto the panelled walls, making faint trellised ghosts. And all these pools of light made shadows of Maggi as she walked. Time and again she caught a flick of movement in the corner of her eye, only to whirl and find that what had moved was some faint silhouette of herself, ponytail and all. It might have been creepy, if it all hadn't been so hot and sleepy.

There were sudden clicks and creaks too, that made her whirl. But there was never anything behind her. And she knew, before she whirled, that it was only the old timbers expanding in the heat. She wasn't a builder's daughter for nothing. It would be spookier in the early evening, when all the timbers contracted again, one after the other, in rows, sounding like pattering ghostly footsteps.

With a deep breath, she stopped before one door; not so very different from the rest, but she had to start somewhere. The keyhole was big, which meant a big key. But they were all big keys. She loosened the strap that held them together, and started trying them one by one, making a pile of the useless ones, as Dad had done.

She tried thirty-seven before one turned. One great big breath, and she went in.

Nothing, except a thick wad of papers in the corner, dark grey with dust. She sifted through them eagerly. But they were all the same. Menus for Christmas dinner, 1957. The Abbey Country Club. She remembered Mr Morris's little smile, with a twinge of hatred.

But December, 1957 . . . seventeen years before she was born. Dad would have been a little boy of ten. Mam only seven, looking forward to Santa Claus, putting notes to him up the chimney. A tear nudged at Maggi's right eye, but she drove it back with a dirty thumb, leaving a big mark in her cheek. Then she noted the number of the key, and wrote that number on the door with a piece of chalk she'd scrounged from Dad's tool-kit.

The next door she settled on was a very grand one, of polished red wood, with great big panels and a gold finger-plate. This time she was lucky; it opened with the seventh key.

This room had two things in it. One was a great baulk of timber, all rough-sawn and hairy, that went vertically up from the floor till it vanished through a jagged black hole in the beautiful gilded ceiling. There was a note pinned to the baulk, in Mr German's spiky writing. 'Placed in position 19-7-87. Do not remove without architect's instructions.' She guessed it was holding up the roof. She felt suddenly hot and bored; this wasn't a secret room. Mr German had been here before her. This room was *spoilt*. She was so disgusted she almost missed the other thing.

A slightly bald teddy bear. He'd been chucked down in the corner, on a swept pile of plaster; on his face, with his bottom in the air. As if he was hiding his eyes from something, or weeping from the loneliness. She picked him up; a great cloud of plaster-dust came from him. He was very long and thin, and the bottoms of his feet were hanging off in flaps. When she squeezed him, he went 'oink'. He had a hunchback, all funny and square.

Anyway, he looked lonely; as if he'd been waiting for her for a very long time. And this was no place for a poor old bear. How many nights had he lain on his own in the dark? And somebody might throw him in the bin at any minute. She tucked him under her arm. She would ask Mzz MacFarlane if she could keep him. Meanwhile, he could be her guide to the Abbey. She decided to call him Mr Abbot.

As she locked the door, she thought she heard somebody singing upstairs; though it was very faint; and when she stopped to listen, she couldn't hear it again. It was probably Mzz MacFarlane, in from the garden . . . it was enough to make Maggi climb another set of stairs, to the second floor.

The next room only opened on the fifty-ninth key; and all it had in it was a pickaxe covered with cement, and some lengths of lead piping. It was very hot, up here on the second floor, close under the roof. She felt a fool, getting all hot and dusty, when she could be in her kitchen drinking a Lilt from the fridge. She decided to try one more door, and then go and have a Lilt.

The seventeenth key, this time. This was the last, though, she thought, before she opened the door.

There was a man in there.

A tall thin man. She couldn't see his face, because he had his back to her, peering out of the window.

She blushed, and blurted out, 'Sorry. Excuse me!'

He didn't take the least bit of notice. He was peering out of the window, left, right, sharp as a cat. He had his arms raised, elbows sticking out. Then he put his head on one side, quick as a snake, and there was a tremendous *crack* that hurt her ears. And a smell like Guy Fawkes' night. Then the man gave a grunt of satisfaction, and said:

'Scream, you crophead . . . cry for your dam, then . . .' in a mumble that sent shivers up Maggi's spine.

Frozen to the spot, Maggi noticed other things. There was a smell of burning. Clouds of brown smoke were drifting past the window. There was a lot of shouting outside. Crackling. The house must be on fire.

She must tell Dad! But, as in a nightmare, she found she couldn't move.

When the man turned from the window, she could've screamed. If he looked up and noticed her . . .

But he didn't look up. He was looking down at a long pole he held in his hands. Or was it a pole? There was a dark glint of metal . . . metal with a wooden end.

He had long greasy hair that fell onto a sleeveless jerkin, like farmhands wore. He had a long leather strap that hung over one shoulder. With little round wooden boxes hanging off it, every few inches. He took one of them and tilted it, and poured powder down the long metal pole. He wore sort of wellies, but they were made of leather, and flopped over at the top.

Then, still not seeing her, he turned back to the window. Picked up an old knife, and scratched a long vertical mark in the plaster on the side of the window. There were four vertical marks already, and a diagonal cross-mark, making a gate-shape. Then he lifted the long metal pole, and poked it out through the window again.

Suddenly, there was a burst of crackling from outside again, like a jumping-jack on Guy Fawkes' night. Then a sharp thud, in the room itself. The man at the window said 'Ah,' and then 'Ah' again, as if he'd made a sudden discovery.

Then the long metal pole went clattering to the floor. He put out his hands, to support himself, one on each side of the window. Then he slowly turned his feet, shuffling slow and soft, to face Maggi.

'Ah,' he said, wisely, again. And the front of his shirt was all red; a red that reached his belt and ran over it, splattering down his trousers like a red waterfall.

His eyes were looking at Maggi, but they still didn't see her. He looked like he was thinking deeply, far away. Then a thin dark trickle came from his mouth, and he fell flat on his face. Once, twice, his left leg kicked. Then it was still, though it quivered a bit.

Then he said 'Ah' for the last time; and a pool of darkness spread and spread across the floorboards towards her.

And Maggi knew no more.

She came to herself. She was lying flat on the dusty floorboards.

She looked for the man.

He wasn't there. There was nothing in the whole room, except Mr Abbot, lying on his nose about three feet away, where she must have dropped him. The window was shut. There were faded roses on the sagging wallpaper. There was no smoke; nobody was shouting outside.

She must've been dreaming; except her right arm hurt a bit, and the side of her face, where she'd fallen.

And she heard voices calling, in the house below.

'Mag-gi! Mag-gi! Where are you?'

Dad's. Mzz MacFarlane's. Mr German's. They sounded a bit worried.

She tried to call out; but her throat was too dry. And it was just too difficult to get up. She simply lay and listened to the voices getting nearer and nearer. Feet pounding on the floorboards; quick worried feet. Then Mr German's voice said, 'She's in here.' His big hands picked her up; his hairy suit scratched her cheek.

'You all right, pet?' asked Dad anxiously. 'Where've you hurt yourself?'

'She must've fainted,' said Mzz MacFarlane. 'It's terribly hot and stuffy in here.'

'There was smoke,' said Maggi, feeling very odd and far away. 'The house was on fire. Men shouting outside. And a man in here. He got hurt. He was bleeding. He was dead.' Her stomach gave a terrible heave, but she managed to keep control of it; just.

'C'mon, love,' said Dad, all embarrassed. 'You're poorly. You've been imagining things. There's no man here!'

'Let's get her downstairs and into bed,' said Mzz MacFarlane. 'I'll take her temperature. She feels sweaty, and her pulse is racing.'

But Mr German said with a frown, 'What did the man look like, Maggi?'

She told him what she could remember. He simply said, 'How odd,' in a calm sort of voice. But Maggi could hear a tremble; she knew he was excited, underneath.

CHAPTER 6

Dad made her stay in bed next morning. She was sure it was Mzz MacFarlane's busybody interfering. There was never any question of staying in bed at home, no matter how rotten she felt. Anyway, Dad said Mzz MacFarlane could cope – not to worry.

The breakfast Mzz MacFarlane fetched her, striding down the long corridor in her sensible flat heels, gave Maggi plenty of cause to worry. The egg was boiled so hard you could've broken a window with it. The toast was burnt, and scraped thin as a biscuit. And there were black bits in the butter, and the tea was grey as the washing-up water.

Maggi supposed she *meant* well.

Afterwards she lay, feeling helpless, useless and cross, her ears desperately trying to suck in any sound coming in through the thick walls that might prove there was life left on earth. The clatter of Mzz MacFarlane washing up. The grunting and groaning of the waterpipes overhead, like a dinosaur with bronchitis. She did *not* want to be left alone today; it was the last thing she wanted. It was amazing how wrong interfering grown-ups could be. Mzz

MacFarlane rabbiting on about her overdoing things, needing rest . . .

Which had left her alone with what she was *really* afraid of. The house. She was afraid of the house now. She had lain awake half the night, listening. Waiting for the house to get into her mind again. All those locked rooms, waiting for her to unlock them.

And – her mind edged up to the thought gingerly, sideways – that man. Who had died and then not been there. She stoutly refused to believe that man had been in *her* mind. That would mean she was going mad. The man was in – the house's mind. Her own mind was perfectly clear, wanting to do the washing up, peel the potatoes, get outside where the sun was shining and the twins shouting, and everything was *ordinary*.

The gentle tap on the door made her jump. It was not a tap she knew. Dad and the twins didn't bother to knock; Mzz MacFarlane's was a brisk policeman's rat-tat.

She was reluctant to shout, 'Come in.' She had no idea what she would be shouting 'come in' to.

Again, the tap. If she kept quiet, it might go away. She snuggled down under the bedclothes. The door opened, very slowly.

She was amazed to see Mr German, in dark green braces and a dark green bow tie. The heat had finally driven him into taking his coat off. His little paunch bulged out his elegant green-striped shirt like half an egg. His bald head, shiny with sweat, also looked like half an egg. He looked a bit like Humpty-Dumpty. She thought he was the strangest-looking person she had ever been alone with. He had a large book under one arm.

'Hallo,' he said, with much too bright a smile. A real three-pound-note job, as Dad would've said. 'I've come to cheer you up. I thought you might be getting bored.'

It was unbelievable. He'd never taken the slightest notice of her before. He couldn't even remember her name, referring to her as 'Annie' or 'Emmie' or 'this young lady'. But now his rather sticky-out blue eyes were bright with a wild excitement. As he pulled up a chair to the bed, and sat much too close to her, she could see his hands were *trembling* with excitement. His sidewhiskers *bristled* with it. She wondered whether he was one of those men they warned you about in school.

But all he did was push the big book towards her, open at a picture of a man in a big white collar, with a very blunt nose and warts all over his face.

'Let's play guessy-games,' said Mr German. 'Guess who that is?'

'Haven't a clue.' She hated not knowing answers.

'It's Oliver Cromwell,' he said playfully. 'I'll bet you've heard of *him*.'

'He cut the King's head off,' she said severely. She did not approve; she was very attached to the Royal Family.

'What else do you know about him?' he asked, slyly, teasingly.

'He had the Roundheads. They smashed windows in churches.' She really didn't know who she liked less, Oliver Cromwell or Mr German.

'Here's a picture of a Roundhead on his horse,' he said ingratiatingly.

'Yes,' she said abruptly.

'And here's one of the men they fought, also on his horse. Do you know what they called those?'

'Cavaliers.' Did he think she was a baby, not to know about Cavaliers and Roundheads?

'How do you think they fought each other?'

'Charged on horseback, I expect.' She didn't like talking about fighting.

'And what did they shoot at each other with? Bows and arrows?'

'If you say so.' She wondered if he really was mad.

'You don't know much about them then? You haven't been doing them at school?'

'Not since juniors. We're doing Bronze Age burials now.'

She darted him a wary look; he was shaking more than ever. Was he going to kill her or rape her? She could hear Dad hammering distantly, up on the roof. The clatter of washing up had long since stopped from the kitchen. She was *quite* alone with him . . .

'What about *this* picture,' said Mr German. She scarcely dared look, she was so scared. Was it him making the bed shake, or her?

But she looked. And gasped. And then felt that all her brains were running out down her neck.

It was the man; the man who had died and then not been there. Same floppy boots, same strap across his shoulder with the little round boxes dangling from it, same long pipe . . . gun . . .

'The man upstairs wasn't wearing a floppy hat,' she gasped. 'But I think it was lying on the floor . . .'

'That's a musketeer of the English Civil War – Cromwell's war. And you'd never seen a picture of one before?'

'No.'

'I had to make sure you hadn't you see. I had to be sure you hadn't made him up. Snipers, they called them – they were the best shots, because they used to go with their guns on the marshes in peacetime and shoot snipe. Snipe are quite small, and they fly terribly fast – so they had to be good shots.'

She suddenly understood all his funny behaviour.

'You were testing me . . . you knew yesterday what I'd seen . . .'

'I had a damned good idea. But I had to be sure. Come on – come upstairs a minute—' He grabbed her hand and hauled her out of bed in her pyjamas, and didn't even wait for her to put on her dressing-gown. But she didn't mind, because his mind was totally on something else.

The little room of yesterday was quite empty. He led her to the window; to the right-hand edge of the window. He pulled back a flap of yellowed rosy wall-paper and there beneath was funny plaster, plaster with black spots in it and shiny black hairs embedded.

And scratched into the plaster, roughly, were four vertical marks and a diagonal crossbar that made them look like a little gate. And then one vertical bar by itself . . .

'Them are the marks the man made!'

'Which you *couldn't* have seen before, because I only tore that wallpaper back this morning.' His voice rose to a squeak with excitement. 'And there's a very dim stain on the floorboards – look – that just might be . . .'

'It's where the blood was,' she said slowly. 'So he really died – he really *was* a ghost.'

'Depends what you mean by ghost.' Mr German

waved his arms about, as if to embrace the whole world. 'Not a ghost that meant you any harm – not a ghost that wanders about scaring people on purpose. More like a tape-recording of a moment in history. All anybody will ever see of him is what *you* saw.'

'I don't want to see it again.' she said abruptly.

'No need. You've done what I need. You've proved for me this house is not just a mouldering Victorian heap. If this room was here in the Civil War – 1642 – it will help us to raise money to save the whole house.'

He began to tear at the yellowed rosy wallpaper. It was damp and came off in great sheets. And great lumps of hairy plaster fell off with it.

And underneath, there were great black crooked beams, set into the wall. Like the sort you saw on country cottages in picture postcards. Mr German went on pulling wallpaper like a lunatic, till the floor was knee-deep. Only then did he sink onto the windowsill, red-faced, sweating and panting. 'Seventeenth century. *This'll* make them sit up and take notice.'

Then he took one of her hands in both this sweating ones. 'Maggi – maybe you can see things other people cannot see . . .'

'Like what?' she quavered, suddenly very frightened.

'Oh, just things that happened . . . a very long time

ago. Will you do me a favour? Just keep your eyes open for anything funny. Maybe they didn't pull the old monastery down. Maybe they just built more and more walls onto it, till they buried it inside what we have now. That happened at Norton Priory, which isn't very far from here. They pulled down a Georgian house, and found bits of the old monastery inside, in the cellars. If you find the same here – they'll have to cough up the money to save the house. I should look myself – but I haven't got time. What with keeping this old roof on, and all the other jobs I've got to see to—' He wiped his cooling face wearily. 'Promise?'

'*Maggi!*' said Dad's voice, very angry, just outside the door of the room. He burst in. '*Why* are you out of bed? What are you doing in your pyjamas, gettin' all filthy? Get back to bed *at once*!'

'It's all right, George,' said Mr German. 'She's helping me. We've found a lot of seventeenth-century walling, good as new.'

But Dad talked right through him, very rudely. 'Maggi, get back to bed at *once*!' She fled. It only occurred to her when she was back in bed that Dad wasn't really angry with her. He was furious with Mr German.

He was still angry as the pair of them walked past her door, five minutes later. She heard Mr German say: 'But it's genuine timber-frame walling, George!'

'Coulda bin put there by the Victorian builders. Brought from somewhere else. Ye knaa how they re-used aad stuff. But waall or no waall Aah'll thank ye to leave our Maggi oot of it. She's ower-imaginative. And she's not ower losin' her mam yet . . .'

This was terrible. Her dad telling his boss off – he'd get the sack and they'd all have to leave, and she couldn't bear it. And Mr German was nice, really, once you got used to his funny ways.

She heard Mr German say goodbye, a bit huffily, then Dad's footsteps came back to her door, and he knocked. Which was worrying, 'cos he never thought to knock usually.

He came and sat on the bottom of her bed, twisting his cap in his hands, head down, with his bald patch showing. After a long silence, and several painfully deep breaths, Dad looked at her and said: 'Ye can forget that rubbish Ted German's been puttin' in your head. There's no such things as ghosts. When people die, they just finish. They go back into the earth. If they go on, they go on as the plants that grow in that earth. An' they go on as memories while people remember them . . .'

He was very pale, and twisted his cap even harder and she knew he was thinking about Mam. Then he said: 'There's a lot of fools reckon different, and there's a lot of sharks who'll tek their money off them

73

by kidding them it's different. Yer Aunty Maude went to them spiritual meetin's after yer mam died, and they told her a lot o' rubbish that yer mam came back and left me a message. Ye know what that message was? Not ter ferget to feed the budgie. We hadn't even got a flippin' budgie by then – it died afore yer mam, though Maude didn't knaa that . . .'

'Dad, I'm sorry.' She leaned over and took his hand.

'Aye, well,' he said roughly, 'just remember. Ye went upstairs yesterday, an' it was aall hot an' stuffy up there, an' yer fell asleep an' had a dream, right? *Right?*'

'Yes, Dad.' What else could she say?

But she knew she hadn't fallen asleep. She knew he was wrong. She knew he was blinding himself, like a racehorse with blinkers over its eyes, so it could only see half of what it should see.

She felt so sorry for him, she started crying.

CHAPTER 7

The trip into Northwich was nothing if not noisy. They went in Mzz MacFarlane's Mini shooting-brake, which was yellow and very rusty, and had green moss growing in all the windowsills. There was a very embarrassing sticker on the back windows that said: TRUST IN THE LORD.

Also, Mzz MacFarlane wasn't half such a careful driver as Dad, and her brakes made terrible noises and only slowed down the car after Maggi had closed her eyes in despair. After one such occasion, a lorry driver leaned out of his cab and shouted, 'I should stop trusting in the Lord, Missus, and have an MOT test!'

'I get tired of that joke,' said Mzz MacFarlane cheerfully. Well, sort of cheerfully.

But most of the time she was being a teacher. She talked non-stop of the habits of grey squirrels, and how they hadn't driven out the red ones, it was all the result of forests being cut down. From squirrels they passed to the cruelties of fox-hunting and badger-digging and the uprooting of hedgerows. She was *quite* interesting, better than the teachers at school, but Maggi thought ruefully she was supposed to be on holiday.

In the launderette, Mzz MacFarlane gave another lecture on the actions of detergents, and how little bits of detergent fastened onto little bits of dirt and pulled them off the clothes. On the way back, it was the awful habits of magpies, and how they ate other birds' eggs, so that if you had magpies you'd never see another bird, but magpies deserved to live too and it was cruel to shoot or poison them . . .

It was only when they were hanging out the washing to dry in the walled garden that Mzz MacFarlane seemed to relax. The walled garden was lovely; high old red brick, glowing in the descending sun, and crab-apple trees fastened to the bricks and climbing up them, in bulging clusters of leaves and fruit. And green grass kept short by two orphaned geese that had appeared from nowhere and been adopted, and Mzz MacFarlane's six free-range hens.

'It's nice, here,' said Maggi, as they finished pegging out, and watched a tiny warm breeze just lifting clothes that looked like Maggi and Mzz MacFarlane, and the twins and Dad, a proper family all blowing on the line.

'Yes, it is,' said Mzz MacFarlane. 'This is my favourite place of all.' And she lifted her eyes half closed to the setting sun, and the breeze blew through her disorganized red hair, and there was really colour in her cheeks. 'But I love all this house . . .'

'Who owns it?' asked Maggi.

'Well, me, actually,' said Mzz MacFarlane. 'I mean, it's for the Marigold Trust. But I put up the money. I sold my parents' house after they were killed, and I had not only enough to buy it, but thirty thousand pounds to repair it, as well. Wasn't that incredible?'

Maggi stared at her in awe. It was terrifying, the idea of owning all those ninety-nine rooms. With so much needing doing. But at least with thirty thousand, she could afford to pay Dad. Thirty thousand seemed an awful lot of money . . .

'I bought it as an act of faith,' said Mzz MacFarlane, dreamily. 'I came up here for a little holiday, after the funeral, and I came across this place and had to have a nosy. And then the idea sort of came to me. The idea of disabled children learning to be market gardeners. I could see the fields of plants, and the wheelchairs whizzing all along the paths, and I didn't want to go back to Jamaica, so I asked how much it was, and it was really amazingly cheap. Less than a three-bedroom semi in London . . .'

'So what do you do for a living now?' asked Maggi.

'I'm the secretary of the Trust. I'm not paid of course. But soon it will all start happening around us. I prayed for an architect, and met Mr German at an architectural class a month later. And he gives his services free. Then I prayed for a site foreman, and your dad turned up, and you as well, to be my little housekeeper. You see, Maggi, prayer really *works*, if you have *faith*. And soon the house will be straight, and the teachers will come, and the children will come. All by *faith*, Maggi! Faith can move *mountains*.'

Maggi backed away. Were all adults bananas in one way or another? Mr German and his spooks, and Dad who wouldn't look at things, and now Mzz MacFarlane using faith instead of money . . .

'Ah well,' said Mzz MacFarlane. 'Nearly supper time. Want any vegetables done?'

CHAPTER 8

Work on the house, announced Mzz MacFarlane, would begin properly next Monday morning, when the Manpower Services Commission were sending nine young trainees along . . .

Dad kept his face straight with an effort.

'What's the matter with trainees?' muttered Maggi, as soon as Mzz MacFarlane swept out.

'Aah'd rather have one old time-served feller than the lot o' them,' said Dad. 'Aah don't care what he is – plumber, carpenter, slater. Just as long as he knows his arse from his elbow.'

'Are they always no good?'

'No, Aah wouldn't go as far as that. Depends whether they've got a good feller in charge. Some of them are good – they built a marvellous full-scale replica of George Stephenson's *Rocket* once, Aah remember. Well, we'll have to take our chance wi' them.'

Maggi's face fell. When Dad talked about taking chances, it was as bad as anybody else threatening to commit suicide.

But it seemed to inspire Dad. As if he wanted to get

everything possible done before some holocaust descended. He nosed round the whole estate, looking for something he called the builder's yard. When he found it, he took Maggi to see it, jubilant. It seemed to contain everything that had ever been left over from building or repairing the great house. Outside, against the wall, were great rows of slates, piles of used brick neatly stacked, and more chimneypots together than Maggi had ever seen before. The yard didn't seem to have been disturbed for years; birds had nested in the chimneypots. Inside a shed were rusty drainpipes and gutters, rows of sheets of glass so dirty you couldn't see through them, tea-chests full of old brass taps and coils of wire, even two lavatory bowls. Everything was covered with spider-webs, so old the spiders had died at their posts; their huge transparent corpses were cheerfully run across by their descendants.

Soon after, minor miracles began to happen. All the sheets of dribbly cardboard that kept the weather out of the kitchen were replaced with glass that was liberally decorated by Dad's thumbprints. Every bare electric bulb was suddenly adorned with an old-fashioned conical white glass lampshade. The smell of new paint and putty was as exciting as the salty smell of the sea at Whitley Bay.

The next miracle was an electric bell for the front door. One morning Maggi saw Mzz MacFarlane counting out notes into Dad's hand. An hour later Dad was up ladders in the corridors, with a coil of grey electric wire round his shoulder that looked long enough for a mountaineer to climb Mount Everest with. An hour after that, Dad screwed a neat white box onto the kitchen wall, and then vanished. Three minutes later, the white box buzzed loudly, and then Dad was back as flushed as a boy, demanding a pint pot of tea.

Then, having installed a new doorbell, he announced he thought he could get the old one to work – the one that worked off the cast-iron handle by the front door.

Maggi was just starting to get the tea when there was a sudden jangle over her head. She jumped a yard in the air, then looked up to see a blackened bell, attached to a board by a long spring, still shaking. Below it, a dingy china plate said 'Front Door'.

She hadn't really looked at that board before, it being stuck right in the corner, high up. But now she noticed there were eleven more bells on springs, marked with names like 'Drawing Room', 'Dining Room', 'Bathroom', and 'Master Bedroom'.

'For summoning the servants,' announced Dad, arriving breathless and ecstatic again. 'They're on springs so they go on waggling once the bell's been rung, so the servants could look up from what they were doing and know which to answer.'

'Could you make them all work?'

'Given time, Aah reckon Aah could. But it wouldn't be worth it. Some of the wires'll be buried in the wall. Besides, we don't know which room is which. Them rooms could be *anywhere* in the house . . .'

But Dad's big triumph was the bathroom. At first they couldn't force the door open more than a foot. Dad poked his head round, and said the bathroom was full of old rusty bicycles. He managed to get one arm through and move the bikes. They got the door open and the bicycles out, and then the bathroom was revealed in all its splendour. The bath was so big you could have swum in it. The bottom was all red with rust, and there were long streaks of rust under the taps. The bath stood on feet like lion's claws.

The ceiling was so high it was nearly out of sight. It had a little skylight in it that gave the only light in the place. But it was the thing on the wall that caught Dad's eye.

'A 1915 Ascot,' he said reverently. 'An Ascot gas geyser. I haven't seen one of those for *years*. I didn't know they had gas here – two miles from the nearest village. Must've cost the earth to put in. Aah wonder if Aah can get it working . . .'

The thing was about six feet high, and shaped a bit like a space rocket, only black.

'Brass, that is,' said Dad. 'Solid brass. An antique, that. They don't make 'em like that any more.'

Maggi was inclined to worry. About escaping gas, and would it blow up, and would Mzz MacFarlane's money last long enough? And yet she couldn't really worry.

Dad was happy again. As happy, it seemed, as when Mam was alive. As happy as a boy on holiday.

After supper, Dad announced, 'Aah've got it working. You can aall have baths tonight. C'mon, see!'

They all filed in, solemnly. The electric light was working, under a regulation conical shade. The floor was revealed as black-and-white marble tiles. The bath was as clean as Vim would make it – a kind of pale orange all over. The taps were highly polished. Dad ran one.

'That's the cold tap, right?'

Then he ran the other. No water came out for a moment. Then there was a terrifying roar behind them, that made them all jump. The whole bathroom shook; flakes of grey whitewash and several live spiders fell into the bath from the ceiling. Maggi spun round; there it was in all its splendour, brass shining like a sergeant-major's belt-buckle, blue flames roaring out of the bottom like it was a Saturn rocket at Cape Kennedy.

'Look,' said Dad. 'Hot water. Without any effort.'

A thin trickle of what looked like strong coffee ran down the end of the bath. But it was steaming; definitely *hot* coffee. The trickle increased to a stream and then to a steam-driven jet like a fireman's hose. The bath rapidly filled with what looked like steaming blood.

'It'll run itself clean, given a bit o' time,' said Dad. 'You want first go, Mzz MacFarlane? You're the lady of the house!'

Mzz MacFarlane went so pale all the freckles showed out across her nose. Mutely she shook her head. Obviously, even her great faith had limits.

It was Maggi who dared it, two hours' running later. The water was cleaner now, just like lemonade shandy. It was nice to have an all-over soak. She stretched out luxuriously and turned on the hot tap again. The *whhoooph* of gas was magnificent. Three more spiders had to be rescued from a hot watery grave.

But she supposed Dad had triumphed again.

CHAPTER 9

'How many cups and mugs is that, Maggi?'
'Twelve, Mzz MacFarlane. And two kettles
boiled ready.'

'I do like these rock cakes you've made. They look
really tasty.'

'Maggi makes a good rock cake mix,' said Dad. 'A
rock for every cake!'

Mzz MacFarlane laughed. She had taken to laughing at Dad's jokes. Which had encouraged him to dig
out all the old ones that went back to Mam's time.
Mzz MacFarlane laughed at them all; even the second
time he told them. What was that a sign of?

And the pair of them had taken to staring at each
other, when the other one wasn't looking. Then catching each other's eye and looking away. Maggi wasn't
certain what that meant, either.

But she had more than that to worry about this
morning. This was the morning the job-creation boys
arrived. This was the morning the Abbey was really
going to start coming back to life.

They were half an hour late already.

'We must give them a nice welcome,' said Mzz

MacFarlane nervously. For the fifth time. 'We must get off on the right foot.' She was dressed in a suit with a skirt for once. She had nice legs, but the hemline was not a fashionable length. Still, Maggi could tell the material was good. And Dad was in his bib-and-brace overalls, with a cap on, a clipboard, and a pencil behind his ear.

Dad looked through the window. 'Here's the minibus now. Aah'll go and fetch them up.'

The first one through the door was a man. He must be the man in charge of the boys. Maggi's heart instantly sank. She somehow *knew* he'd been a teacher; and she somehow *knew* he hadn't been a successful one. For one thing, he wore a bobble hat. For another, he wore a bright red shirt and tie, and horn-rimmed glasses, with a row of pens in the breast pocket of his sports coat. He blinked round warily, as if expecting someone to throw something at him; then ignored Mzz MacFarlane and came straight across to Maggi, enclosing her hand in a hand like a warm Yorkshire pudding.

'My name's Jack Timmins,' he said. 'You can call me Jack. Everybody calls me Jack.' You could see he thought he was good with children; and you could see he would be really terrible, the sort they took the mickey out of.

'Good morning, Mr Timmins,' said both Dad and

Mzz MacFarlane together. Then looked at each other in confusion.

At that point a distant shouting and scuffling that had been approaching reached the door, and the boys burst in. The first, a tall bulky red-head, blundered straight into Mr Timmins's back on purpose, sending him staggering.

'Hey up, Timmins, you're in't road!' He sat on the table with a thump, making it shake, and began to finger the rock buns. The rest barged in after him and sat down on every chair and windowsill without being invited. Two of them began an arm-wrestling match over a half-eaten apple.

In a second, it had ceased to be her kitchen, Dad's kitchen, Mzz MacFarlane's kitchen; it had become the worst kind of classroom. Mzz MacFarlane stepped forward, a patch of red burning in each cheek, and began her speech of welcome.

The awful boys didn't take a blind bit of notice; just went on talking, swinging their legs and squabbling over the apple. Mzz MacFarlane went on and on and on, then her voice began to falter. Mr Timmins just stood staring at the floor, as if everything was quite normal.

'Shut up,' said Dad suddenly. Then again. 'SHUT UP!' It was his army voice; his sergeant's voice.

A deathly hush fell; everyone became aware that

Dad was glaring at the red-haired boy, and the red-haired boy was glaring back at Dad. It was the boy's eyes dropped first; after a long struggle. Instead, he picked up a rock bun and began to eat it.

'PUT THAT BUN DOWN!' Dad's voice was so grating it sounded like an old door opening.

'Ye what?' said the red-haired boy, through a mouthful of bun. Crumbs trickled down his faded blue anorak.

'You heard what I said. Put–that–bun–down.'

'Make me!'

Dad walked across. The pair of them swayed, in another bout of arm-wrestling. Then Dad had prised the boy's fingers apart, and put the bun back on the plate.

'There's no need for physical violence,' said Mr Timmins, sounding as miffed as if he'd backed the loser in the four-thirty. 'After all, these boys are volunteers . . .'

'They're gettin' paid, aren't they?' said Dad.

'A pitiful amount. They are being exploited by the capitalist system.'

'An' part of that exploitation is listening to what the lady's saying. Now shut up, an' *listen*!'

There was a silence, of sorts. All the boys stared at the floor, or at their own swinging feet. Mzz MacFarlane started again; but her voice was shaky now.

'As I was saying, I'd like to welcome you on behalf of the Marigold Trust. I just want to put you in the picture about what we're trying to achieve here. We are going to turn this house into a school where young people who are confined to wheelchairs can be taught to earn their own living and be independent by working in horticulture . . . er, market gardening . . .'

'Flaming spastics,' muttered the red-haired boy loudly.

'THAT'S IT!' said Dad, even more loudly. 'Out – the lot of you. Gather on the forecourt outside and we'll try to get you started being useful for a change.'

Mzz MacFarlane just stood, on the verge of tears. Then she grabbed the plate of rock buns and offered them to the departing boys. 'Please – take one – they were meant for you.'

Heads down, each boy grabbed one as he passed. When the last boy was gone, Mzz MacFarlane ran to the door, as if longing to bring them back and try a fresh start.

Then she returned, white faced. 'They've dropped the rock buns all over the gallery floor. They were throwing them at each other and kicking them around . . .'

'What do you expect?' asked Mr Timmins, waspishly. 'You offered them violence – institutionalized violence. And they've returned that violence in their own way. And I for one don't blame them.'

Dad made a sound of deep disgust in his throat; like he was going to spit, except he didn't. 'Aah'll get after them, afore they mess up anything else.'

'Let me tell you – your old-fashioned methods won't work with these boys,' said Mr Timmins. 'They are the new poor – underprivileged in a consumer-orientated society whose rewards they are barred from sharing, through no fault of their own. They need careful handling . . .'

'They need a good boot up the backside,' said Dad, and went, closely followed by Mr Timmins. They listened to that bleating voice receding. Then Mzz MacFarlane sighed and fell into a chair.

'I had such *hopes*,' she said, bleakly.

'I'll clear up the gallery,' said Maggi. She couldn't bear to go on looking at Mzz MacFarlane's face.

Dad came back at lunch time, looking pretty worn round the edges. 'They're having their lunch in the mini-bus. At least if they wreck that, it's no skin off our noses. You can't turn your back for a second. If they're not throwing stones at the statues, they're breaking branches off the trees.'

'They can't be all like that, surely!' said Mzz MacFarlane stoutly.

'We-ell, no,' said Dad. 'There's three or four quiet

ones that seem a bit scared of the rest. Ye might do something wi' them, if you got them away from Timmins and that ginger freak Stuttwick.'

'I'll take them weeding the rose beds after lunch,' said Mzz MacFarlane, brightening up. 'Try to get to know them. What'll you do with the rest?'

'We're filling potholes in the drive from the gravel heap. Aah daren't let them inside the house. What we'll do if it rains . . .'

'Perhaps they'll settle down once they get used to us?'

'They'd settle if we got rid of Timmins and Stuttwick.'

'Manpower Services don't let you pick and choose.'

'Mebbe Aah'll take them up on the roof. Timmins an' Stuttwick might fall off.'

'You are awful, Mr Adams. A proper Tory land-lord.'

'Me – Tory?' yelped Dad. 'Never voted Tory in me life. Solid Labour – though Aah'm startin' to have me doubts. Now Aah would've thought you were the Tory, Mzz MacFarlane, a lady like you . . .'

'Never in my life. Our family have been Liberals since the year dot. Great-great-grandfather was in Gladstone's last cabinet.'

'Waste of time voting for the Alliance.'

And the pair of them were off, bickering like a

couple of kids and both loving it. Maggi looked at Dad's face, as she cleared up his dirty plate and mug from round him. He hadn't been so alive for years. She did the washing up, just glad he was happy.

Until the sound of something else breaking, floating through the open window, got him out of his seat and pounding downstairs.

CHAPTER 10

Maggi surveyed the kitchen with satisfaction. For once, in the absence of Dad and the twins, she'd got it spotless. Every work surface gleamed. The plums were cooling in their glass bowl on the windowsill. The custard had set nicely; not too hard, which Dad hated; not too runny, which the twins hated. The oven chips were nearly done, and the bought pies ready to slip in to warm up. She glanced at the big kitchen clock, which Dad had got ticking. Half past six. Spot on tea time. And it was Gaz's turn to lay the table.

The evening sun, streaming across the grey kitchen wall in lovely diagonal patterns, drew her to the window. She breathed in the scent of warm Cheshire evening, and looked down on the rose garden. Mzz MacFarlane, hair done up in a headscarf, was still weeding. She'd nearly won her battle; eighteen rose beds lay behind her, neat raked bare soil. Only two lay ahead, knee-deep in groundsel and docks. Mzz MacFarlane poked with her trowel severely; removed weeds with strong determined twists of her thin wrists; like a schoolteacher reducing a class to order.

From this distance, Maggi loved Mzz MacFarlane; or maybe it was just the peaceful sunny long-shadowed evening, making her love everything. She loved Mzz MacFarlane enough to wonder whether she was happy. Must be ever so odd to have no mam, no dad, not even a feller interested. She didn't look happy; but then she didn't look unhappy either. Just busy; maybe satisfied getting her way with the rose garden.

Then the old black telephone rang. Maggi, with a sinking heart, just knew it must be Dad. Nobody else rang the Abbey after five, and hardly anybody before that. And she knew before she lifted the phone what had happened. The *QE2* had broken down again. The oven chips would be *ruined*; either cold and soggy, or charred to a cinder. She told Dad, narky, that the chips would be ruined.

Dad said cheerfully that she sounded just like her mam. He also said they were still in Chester; that he'd got the load of second-hand planks at the right price, and that the twins had enjoyed the bike shops. And he would soon fix the *QE2*.

'Pigs might fly!' she snapped, and slammed the phone down. She might as well feed herself and Mzz MacFarlane; no point in spoiling all the oven chips. She called to her, through the open window. Mzz MacFarlane only heard her third shout. Her thoughts must've been miles away. Maggi even began to doubt the crouching figure *was* Mzz MacFarlane . . .

It took Mzz MacFarlane nearly half an hour to get round the house, put her tools away and get washed and changed. In this house, everything was so far away from everything else. The oven chips were like crisps by that time. But Mzz MacFarlane had brought her a huge bunch of wild flowers, culled from the rose bed. Touched, Maggi put them in the big brown jug and set them on the table.

It was a lively tea time; oven chips bounced all over the tablecloth as they tried to spear them. Suddenly they were both giggling like silly girls. Mzz MacFarlane was really quite human.

Then she spoiled it by giving a lecture on the Latin names of the wild flowers in the jug. By the time she was finished, Maggi really hated the flowers.

But they sat on and on, as the sky clouded over, and the warm August dusk began to peer in at the windows. Mzz MacFarlane jumped up suddenly and said, 'Let's have some light on the subject!'

But the lights only made things worse; it made it suddenly night outside. And suddenly, in her mind, the dark empty rooms around them stirred into life. It was night: the house's time; she and Mzz MacFarlane and their little patch of light were lost in the dark belly of the house.

The phone rang, making them both jump. Dad, sounding tired and cross. He'd checked the points and plugs and timing. It must be a blockage in the fuel-pipe.

'Aah'll probably be home by midnight, pet!'

She put the phone down very slowly; even after he had hung up. She wanted that much to be near him . . .

'Want a hand with the washing up?' said Mzz MacFarlane.

'No, there's not much, thanks.' She wanted to spin it out, to fill in the time till Dad came. She scraped the charred corpses of the oven chips into the bin.

'I'll go and do some typing, then. *More* appeal letters.'

Afterwards, Maggi tried to settle to an old *Woman's Realm* of 1976. But she just read the same stupid paragraph about treacle tarts over and over again. The light in the kitchen seemed to get dimmer and dimmer, as if someone was trying to strangle the light bulb. The thin, often-stopping chatter of Mzz MacFarlane's typewriter was her only lifeline. And her mind roamed the empty rooms. She just *knew* something was going to happen.

When it did, it was horrible.

A terrible screeching; a bellowing in agony that filled the house. Like someone being tortured to death. Except it didn't sound *human*. A person screaming would've been a relief.

Mzz MacFarlane's footsteps, running. Mzz MacFarlane, white and shaking, crying, 'What is it? What *is* it?' Then she grabbed Maggi's hands, saying: 'Don't worry, Maggi. I'm sure there's some sensible explanation.' But the trembling in her big gardening-roughened hands was worse than the bellowing.

The terrible noise seemed to be getting nearer, coming up the corridor towards them.

'Lock the door, *please*, miss!' Mzz MacFarlane fumbled so long with the keys that in the end Maggi tried to grab them off her, and they fought for them yelling, as if they hated each other.

Then the key was found; the door locked.

The awful noise seemed to retreat. Then get nearer again. Then retreat again.

Finally, Mzz MacFarlane said, 'I can't stand any-more of this. I'm going to find out what it *is*.'

'Oh, miss, don't, don't, it'll get you . . .'

But Mzz MacFarlane had grabbed up Dad's big torch and was heading for the door, undoing the lock like she was crazy.

It was a case of follow her or be left alone with the noise.

Maggi followed. On her way out she picked up the big sharp breadknife. It was a bit of a comfort. She was just in time to see Mzz MacFarlane turn the corner. At least, in the dim lights of the long corridor she *thought* it was Mzz MacFarlane . . . she ran after her, to make sure. But all she could see when she reached the corner was a shadow vanishing down the great staircase.

She followed; terror in front of her and terror behind, and all the time that terrible inhuman noise bellowed up and down the corridors. She felt helpless, like in a nightmare. All she could do was run on blindly. But there was *someone* turning on the lights in the corridors ahead.

Until suddenly all the lights went out together . . .

'Mzz MACFARLANE!' No reply. 'MZZ MACFARLANE!' Only the echoing corridors mocked her.

Then a hand grabbed her and said crossly, 'I'm here, silly. Shut up. I've found the noise. It's coming from this cupboard.'

The cupboard was the one at the end of the bottom corridor; huge and flimsy, and painted with dark, scarred varnish. And certainly the dreadful noise was coming from it. Except when they opened it, it was quite empty, except for an old drum of Vim and a rusty dustpan that had once been pale blue.

'Whatever it *is*,' gritted Mzz MacFarlane, 'is behind this cupboard. I'm . . . going . . . to . . . try . . .

and . . . move . . . it. Hold the torch steady!'

'Miss, please leave it where it is. It can't do us any harm if it's locked in there . . .'

But Mzz MacFarlane wasn't even listening. 'I'm – going–to–get–to–the–bottom–of–this–if–it–*kills*–me.'

A kind of fatal calm gripped Maggi. She'd seen this scene so often in the horror movies she watched on telly, hugging a cushion, terrified, after the twins had finally gone to bed and Dad was out working late. The monster always arrived, and some person went crazy and couldn't bear it, and ran straight into the monster's jaws. She wondered sadly who would look after Dad once the monster had ripped both her and Mzz MacFarlane to bits. She hoped there'd be enough bits of her left so she could be buried in the church-yard at home beside Mam . . .

Under the impact of Mzz MacFarlane's frenzied muscles, the cupboard screeched on the stone floor, and gave at one side. A black gap opened, big enough to slip through.

And beyond was what she had all along expected. A door straight out of a Dracula movie, pointed at the top, and with huge rusting hinges, and horrible white fungus dribbling down it, glistening. And a smell of pure rotting evil, of tombs and crypts and churchyard decay . . .

'Just dry rot,' said Mzz MacFarlane, stoutly. 'The

fruiting head of dry rot fungus.' Maybe it *was* dry rot, which Dad often talked about. At least the fungus lay quite still, just oozing drops of evil liquid in the light of the torch. It didn't even start spreading across Mzz MacFarlane's hands as she clutched at the door . . . maybe the door would be locked . . . she *prayed* it might be locked.

But it swung open with that evil groaning screech they used in the horror movies. And, of course, there was a flight of steps, shiny with damp, leading down . . .

'Miss, *please* don't go down . . .'

But Mzz MacFarlane stepped down, as if drawn by an irresistible evil force; and Maggi had no choice but to slither down after her.

A long brick tunnel lay ahead; a curving roof of brick overhead. And from the brick hung long white strands like an old man's wispy beard, moving slowly in a draught, as if it reached out for their faces.

'Dry rot cilia,' snapped Mzz MacFarlane. 'Just brush it aside. It won't kill you.' She walked straight into the waiting curtains of it. And didn't suddenly scream and writhe and turn to jelly on the floor.

So holding her breath, as the torch dwindled away in front of her, Maggi followed. The tendrils brushed her face and hands like graveyard fingers. Her face was covered with it, so that she breathed it in, because she had to breathe or *burst*.

She suddenly bumped into something. But it was only Mzz MacFarlane's back.

Mzz MacFarlane had stopped because there was a corner; a turn to the right. And now, from that corner came the most dreadful and loud burst of devilish noise yet.

'Oh, come *on*,' yelled Mzz MacFarlane. And *went*. And giving up all hope; giving up her soul to her maker; giving her body to be torn to pieces; Maggi went after her.

She saw, in the light of the torch, and through the glistening waving strands of white, a thousand points of light watching her, unwavering. She just had time to tell herself they weren't rats' eyes, because rats' eyes were red, and these were green.

'Wine racks,' said Mzz MacFarlane raspingly. 'Hundreds of bottles. Quite undrinkable, I expect.'

Then something white moved, beyond the racks.

A long white face, a straggly beard, oblong, hate-filled eyes . . .

'That *ghastly* goat again,' yelled Mzz MacFarlane. 'How on earth did it get down here?' She swung the torch upwards. 'Oh, look, a sloping airshaft. It must have fallen down, stupid thing.'

The nanny goat, almost as if caught out like a naughty schoolgirl, moved forward and let herself be caught by the leather loop round her neck. She brayed again; it echoed terribly in the confined space. Then they were both laughing helplessly. Maggi felt the terror running out of her legs like someone had pulled a plug out of the bath.

Then Dad's voice echoing down the cellar steps.

'What the heck's going on?'

'I thought it might be the goat all along,' said Mzz MacFarlane. The adult world was picking itself up and putting on a brave face again.

'You've blown the fuses again. I told you not to switch on too many lights at once,' Dad grumbled.

Then everyone was talking at once, and laughing their heads off about the goat. But Maggi had a feeling it was a lot more than a lost goat. The house had revealed itself to her again.

She tried not to think of dirty old men in raincoats.

But, maybe this cellar *was* the medieval monastery, like Mr German had hoped. She'd better ring him straight away. The thought should have cheered her up.

But it didn't.

CHAPTER 11

'Nope,' said Mr German. 'No way. These cellars are solid Victorian. Given over to the worship of the god of wine. Same construction as Victorian sewers and railway tunnels.'

But Maggi was so fed up she wasn't listening. After a while, even Mr German noticed, and said, as if he was offering her a consolation sweet: 'You were right about the Cavaliers and Roundheads, though. I've been to the County Records Office, and there *was* a battle here, in 1644 – well, a siege, anyway. The Abbey was held for the King, and the Roundheads came up from Nantwich. It only lasted a morning, then the house surrendered. But there were people killed on both sides, and one wing of the house caught fire, and was burnt down. I'm going to contact the Sealed Knot, and try to get them to re-stage the siege, next spring. Could give the Marigold Trust a bit of publicity, which won't do any harm. Help the fund-raising . . .'

Maggi was appalled. Men had died here; died in agony. And all Mr German could do was to prattle on about fund-raising. She saw again the dying man's baffled face, and thought people were very heartless.

'Well, must be off,' said Mr German, consulting his watch. 'I'm late on site at Crewe as it is. And they're *paying* me there. We're turning a disused church into a picturesque ruin, and I've got all the lovely slates for another job I'm on . . .'

At least he helped her slide the varnished cupboard back. When the sound of his car faded, she felt lonely. She didn't even know if she was alone in the house. Dad had the job-creation lads out in the woods, where they could do least harm. And she *thought* Mzz MacFarlane had gone into Northwich. But several times, before Mr German had come, she'd thought she'd heard somebody singing upstairs. Though surely the doorbell would've fetched Mzz MacFarlane down, if she had been upstairs? Anyway, you couldn't waste the whole day wandering about finding out where people were. There was cooking to do. Toad-in-the-hole tonight. She just hoped the twins never twigged how scared she was of being alone in the house. If they started hiding and jumping out of dark corners, they'd give her a heart attack. Like Mam . . .

The doorbell going was bad enough. First the new one, and then, before she could even move, the old one. Then the new one again. Someone was in a huge hurry . . . had someone been hurt in the woods? She ran downstairs, and arrived breathless.

It was a total stranger. A Hell's Angel. Except he was rather *old* for a Hell's Angel. His face was all deep lines, which seemed to be filled up with dark engine oil. *And* the deep pores of his nose and cheeks. His leather jacket was so filthy that it didn't shine at all. It was a very large jacket, with a very large man inside it. She thought of the phrase 'built like a barn door'. She'd never believed it, but it was true.

He had taken his helmet off, and held it under one arm. The helmet was all motorbike stickers, but they were faded and half scratched off. The removal of the helmet revealed a short-back-and-sides haircut. The skin under the short-back-and-sides was paler and cleaner than the skin of his face.

'Logs,' said the oily face, exposing very yellow teeth, with some missing. 'Want any logs for the fire, little missus?'

All she could think of to say, as the August heat swept in from the gravel of the forecourt, was, 'It's a bit too hot for fires.'

'Aye. That's what they all say. You could save the logs up for next winter. Winters get very cold round here. I could give you a discount. Ninety pence a sack?'

His voice wasn't really at all like a Hell's Angel's. It was weary and very discouraged, like Dad when he was at his worst. And old-fashioned, respectful. She looked at him again. He must be much older than

Dad. She suddenly felt sorry for him. And she had housekeeping money upstairs. Mzz MacFarlane *might* need logs some time.

'Can I see the logs?' she said, carefully.

He waved a large oily hand. On the gravel, a motor-bike and sidecar were parked. Only the sidecar was merely a long home-made wooden box, a bit like a coffin. It contained four plastic bags full of logs, and a rather large and cramped-looking Alsatian dog, who looked acutely and painfully on his best behaviour.

'This is Wolf,' said the Hell's Angel. 'Give the lady your paw, Wolf. Shek' hands.'

The dog lifted its paw, with an air of long, patient endurance. Maggi thought it was, like the man, very big and powerful and yet . . . losing hope. What Dad called 'over the hill'.

'He doesn't like ridin' in the sidecar. But I daren't leave him at home. I'm divorced, an' I've got to lodge wi' me sister, and me brother-in-law can't stand the dog. He's always threatening to take him out an' shoot him, when me back's turned . . .'

'I'll take four bags of logs,' said Maggi suddenly. 'That'll be three pounds sixty?' She just prayed she had that much money left.

'Three pounds sixty it is, little missus.' The man cheered up visibly. 'Where d'you want them put?'

Maggi showed him the little door at the base of the

clock tower, where there was already coal kept. He carried two bags at once, one under each arm; but by the time he was finished he was sweating, and licking his lips like he was dry. A sunlit sadness suddenly made her ask, 'Would you like a mug of tea?'

'I would that! And could I have a bowl of water for Wolf?'

She led the way. He made such a point of wiping his oily boots on the old doormat she thought it was going to collapse into shreds. She almost expected the Alsatian to wipe its paws. She knew she was breaking every rule, asking a strange man into an empty house but . . .

She heard the singing upstairs again, and that made it seem all right.

'Someone's got a good voice,' said the man.

'That's Mzz MacFarlane, the lady who owns the house.'

'Grand place!' The man gazed about him in awe. 'I've often driven past this place, but I never thought to see inside.'

She gave Wolf water in a glass pudding-basin, and put the kettle on, and then, horribly, could think of nothing more to say. But the man had no such worries.

'Me name's Percy. Percy Sandbach. Live in Winsford. I've always had animals, dogs and cats. Me feyther had a small-holdin'. There were always stray cats turning up. We had a cheeky one, just walked straight intut kitchen, and settled on't hearthrug. Me feyther said, after a week, "Percy, I'll have that cat drownded." So I took out cat and drowned her, and went back to kitchen. An' within five minutes, that cat were back again, in her old place soppin' wet washing herself dry. So I said to me feyther, "Feyther, I've drowned that cat once, I'll not drown her again." So we called her Emily an' she lived to be eighteen.'

Or again, he would drift to the sink and turn the dripping tap off. And when it wouldn't stop dripping, he'd say, 'That needs seeing to!'

Or again, 'You know why your beech trees are dyin'? 'Cos courting couples is parking under them of a night, an' crushin' the roots. You want a good gate on your drive, an' a feller in the lodge . . .' And he wasn't being bossy, just matter-of-fact.

The sunlight streamed in through the windows; Wolf lay by the stove with his nose between his paws, as if he had lived in the house for ever; and Percy rambled gently through his life, only pausing to ask for another mug of tea. It was unreal. Percy should be on his way, selling more logs. She should be getting on with the toad-in-the-hole. She ought to be *worried* with this terrifyingly huge man in the kitchen.

But it was so peaceful. And she kept hearing the

singing upstairs, and expecting that at any minute, Mzz MacFarlane would come down and break things up.

And then Mzz MacFarlane did come.

Up the drive in her Mini, with her typical sharp toot-toot to let people know she was home.

So who was singing upstairs?

But what could she possibly say, and not sound as if she was going bonkers?

And when Mzz MacFarlane was in the room, and Percy was introduced as the man who sold logs, and the talk fell to trees and courting couples and soon Mzz MacFarlane was just sitting listening as well.

And then Dad came in, furious with the job-creation lads again.

'Aah can't keep me eye on all of them, all the time . . .'

'That's not a civvie voice,' said Percy. 'Not a civvie haircut.'

Dad looked at him, furious for a minute at being interrupted. Then he grinned and said, 'That's not a civvie voice or a civvie haircut either!'

'Sergeant, REME,' said Percy. 'Aden an' Borneo.'

'Sergeant, RE,' said Dad. 'Germany an' Gib!'

'Put it there,' said Percy, holding out an oily paw. And put it there Dad did, grinning like a boy.

And then there were more mugs of tea, and more

grumbles about job-creation boys and courting couples and dogs and brothers-in-law, and logs and trees and courting couples . . . and somehow, by the end of it, Percy was coming to work at the Abbey, to supervise the trees and the boys, and to live in the half-ruined gatehouse and keep out the courting couples.

After he had finally gone, and Maggi turned her hands to the toad-in-the-hole, she heard Mzz MacFarlane say to Dad, 'You see, we got someone to help you. We've just *got* to have faith . . . it's uncanny the way things have turned up as I needed them.'

But all Maggi could think of was Wolf. Wolf was a sort of lost dog, and Percy was a sort of lost dog. And in her own way, Mzz MacFarlane was a sort of lost dog. And Mr German, desperate to find his lost abbey.

And even Dad . . .

Were *all* adults really lost dogs, once you saw them clearly? And if not, why did the lost dogs keep on turning up at the Abbey? Almost as if the Abbey was drawing them in like a magnet?

And, remembering the voice upstairs, suddenly she was afraid.

CHAPTER 12

'What's frettin' you?' Dad asked suddenly, putting down a carefully dried plate.

It amazed Maggi that he'd noticed. It showed how much better he was, since they'd come here. A month ago, he hadn't even noticed when she'd been crying . . .

She was silent a long time; it was such a stupid thing that was worrying her; stupid once you put it into words, anyway. But they were alone in the sunlit kitchen, because the twins had slipped out without washing up again, and it was cosy together. So she said, 'It's Percy and his dog . . .'

'The dog bin' frightening you or *what*?' She knew what the 'what' meant, even if Dad could never put it into words. She felt the quick rage rise in him.

'No, no. I like Percy and I like Wolf.'

'What, then?'

'We-ell, Wolf's a bit of a lost dog . . . he's getting a bit old and tired and he's sort of lost. And Percy is a bit of a lost dog as well and . . . Mzz MacFarlane. And the house is sort of drawing them all in. Even us. And I keep wondering what it *wants* us for.'

He was silent for so long she gave him a furtive glance.

He was grinning. 'So I'm a lost dog as well?'

'Not now. You were before we came here.'

'Aye,' he said, still grinning. 'By, you're gettin' a sharp one, our Maggi. But Aah'll tell ye a secret. The world's full o' lost dogs. And when ye get a funny job like this one, it does draw them in. Any big construction site, the motorways, the oil rigs, they all draw in lost dogs. Divorced fellers, drunks, fellers on the run. Happy men stay home with their wives, you see?'

'Yes.' Now she felt stupid.

'What's more, how come Percy started workin' here? Who encouraged him? Who had him upstairs for a mug o' tea? Kept him here till we came back?'

'Me.'

'Aye. Just like yer mam. She was always lookin' after lost dogs as well.'

It all seemed so simple, in that sunlit kitchen.

'How's that poor man making out at the lodge?' asked Mzz MacFarlane, the following lunch time. 'The place is such a wreck, I feel ashamed. Wouldn't he be happier living up here with us?'

'Not on your life,' said Dad. 'We did the loose slates on his roof. He's got a good log fire blazin' in his chimney, to dry the place out. Aah took him a few spare blankets. He's not got much in the world, apart from that dog an' his power-saw for logs. But he's doin' wonders with old chairs an packin' cases. He's as happy as a sandboy – reckon the pair of them had a pretty rough time at his sister's.'

'I like his new gate across the drive – that red and white pole thing.'

'Real army style, that!'

'He gave me a salute when he opened it for me this morning—'

'It's put paid to the courtin' couples an' vandals . . . he had a bit o' bother at first, but one look at Wolf an' they changed their minds. Wolf and him's quietened down that job-creation lot as well.'

'So it seems. Mr Timmins accused me yesterday of terrorizing them with ex-army thugs and killer dogs.'

Everyone stared, open-mouthed. Mzz MacFarlane had made a joke! Everyone laughed; it was warm and snug like a real family.

When they'd all trailed off back to work, and the kitchen was tidy, Maggi put her sewing things and a pair of Dad's jeans into an old basket, added her faithful copy of *Woman's Realm* and set out for the rose garden.

The iron gate was still wired up against the goats;

but there wasn't a goat in sight as she undid the wire and slipped through. The sunlit silence was not lonely. She could hear Dad's hammer banging away somewhere, high up. He was somewhere where there was an echo; each blow of the hammer came to her three times, getting fainter and fainter. On the fringe of the wood, the twins climbed a fallen beech trunk, looking tiny and sharp as ants. Further into the wood, she heard the thin wail of Percy's power-saw. If they were going to be short of anything this autumn, it would not be logs for the fires. Otherwise, it was peace-day, the day the job-creation boys spent at college.

Mzz MacFarlane had weeded the rose beds, but hadn't had the heart to prune the roses. Each bush was as high as a small tree; their long rose-laden branches waved in the slightest warm breeze, and tangled together over the paths, to form tunnels, some so narrow you couldn't squeeze through without getting scratched. It made the rose garden into a sort of maze. And in the middle of the maze was a circular clearing, with an old sundial, and an even older stone bench. There might once have been lions' heads carved on the ends of the bench; but they were so worn with the wind and rain she couldn't be sure they weren't just rough bits of stone.

It was what Dad called a sun trap; her favourite place; the place where she had always felt safest and most loved, ever since the first night they came. And it was secret; it wasn't a place the twins could find her, and demand instant grub; or even Dad, wanting a cup of tea. For once he could make it for himself . . .

The old seat was mossy; but the moss was warm and brown and dry in the sun, like a cushion. She settled comfortably.

By the time she noticed the voice, it had been singing for some time, without her really noticing. In the beginning it was so faint it might not have been in the rose garden at all. A happy sort of voice, humming and singing sleepily to itself, just part of the sunny drowsy afternoon. The tune was strange to her, monotonous and yet pleasant, as if it was a song with many verses and many choruses. Certainly it wasn't a pop song, not even one of Dad's golden oldies from the sixties. Not even like the classical songs the music teacher played at school; or the songs Gran liked to sing on her coach trips. For some reason, it reminded her of Christmas. How odd, to be sitting here in the baking sun, thinking of Christmas!

The song grew a little louder, as if the singer was drawing nearer. It was one of those voices you some-times got on the radio, when you couldn't tell if the singer was a deep-voiced woman, or a shrill man. Maybe it *was* Mzz MacFarlane, still weeding. She'd never heard Mzz MacFarlane sing. But she must know some pretty weird songs, having been out in Jamaica and Sri Lanka.

And the way the voice kept moving about the rose garden in short sharp darts, with pauses in between when it was stationary, did make it sound like somebody weeding, or snipping off dead rose heads, or cutting roses for her endless jam jars. Maggi kept very still; to make Mzz MacFarlane jump, when she finally arrived. Maybe Mzz MacFarlane would be happy, and not start a lecture . . . and they could have a nice talk or a good laugh . . .

So it was disconcerting to hear a window being pushed open on the top floor of the house and, looking up, see Mzz MacFarlane herself leaning out, beating clouds of dust out of a small piece of carpet. Mzz MacFarlane saw her, and waved.

'Hellooooh, Maggi! Having a bit of peace and quiet, all by yourself? Don't blame you. I'd come and join you, if I wasn't so busy.'

The window slammed down again, leaving Maggi feeling suddenly very lonely. Even though the voice was now quite close.

If Mzz MacFarlane had seen Maggi, why hadn't she seen the owner of the voice? Why hadn't she called out, 'Who's your friend?' or, 'I see you've got company!'

Because the owner of the voice was certainly there;

you couldn't have imagined it. It was no further off than the far side of the rose bed behind her. She could even hear the voice breathing, with a little catch of breath between the words. And yet . . .

No sound of footsteps crunching on the gravel.

She told herself not to be silly. It must be some young gardener Mzz MacFarlane had hired from the village. Wearing soft plimsolls . . .

So why was she cowering down behind the back of the seat; trying to hold her breath until she nearly burst? Desperately telling herself it was a *nice* voice, a *harmless* voice, a voice lost in its own happiness?

The voice came on, to the very entrance of the place where she sat. She summoned up every ounce of courage, and *looked*.

But there was nothing in the gap; and the voice was moving away again.

Immediately, her fear turned into curiosity. She ran to the gap and looked left, the way the voice had gone.

Nothing. But it was still sounding, further off. She quickened her pace, pushing aside the rose branches that clutched at her. But at the next corner, nothing again. It led her round and round the paths of the rose garden that were like a maze.

And then the voice was outside the garden altogether, beyond the old brick wall.

By the time she'd undone the wire on the gate, the

voice had drifted round the corner of the house. And when she reached the corner, it was still moving away behind the box hedge that backed the white statues. She ran on to the next corner, panting.

Only to hear the voice echoing from the great open door of the Abbey.

And in the doorway, she heard it drifting up the great staircase.

And on the stairs, she heard it in the first-floor corridor.

And in the first-floor corridor, she heard it echoing through the ceiling from the second-floor corridor.

And in the second-floor corridor, she could hear nothing, except the gentle sighing of the wind. Nothing moved. Except a piece of loose wallpaper fluttering in the warm draught that came from the open window at the far end. She reached out, ever her mother's daughter, to smooth the wallpaper back into place. But it came away in her hand.

Underneath was black oak; where two heavy beams fitted together. There was something carved in the beam.

But it was just 'LXXIII'. She knew that was the Roman numeral for '73'. What a boring thing to carve, if you had to carve graffiti!

The funny thing was, the other beam, that fitted into it, also had 'LXXIII' carved on it.

Daft. Pointless. Stupid boys . . . she picked up the offending piece of wallpaper, spat on it, and slammed it back into place. It stuck, sort of.

Then a door just beside her opened without warning, and a figure stepped out. But before Maggi could scream, she saw it had tangled red hair.

'Maggi! You look like you've seen a ghost! Did you want me for something?'

'Did you hear somebody singing, just now?'

'What kind of singing?'

'A funny monotonous song. A sort of nonsense song. The only words I could make out were "day us" and something like "Or rabbit".'

'You mean . . . a song like this?'

And Mzz MacFarlane began to sing a song very like the song she had heard in the garden. But her voice was quite different from the voice in the garden.

'Please, miss, what *is* it?'

'Medieval plain-chant. In Latin, of course.'

'Did you *do* Latin?'

'We had to, at boarding school. Enough to know that "Day us" – "deus" – is Latin for "God". And that your "or rabbit" sounds like the Latin "orabit" – "he has prayed".'

'Oh, miss. Was that singing the ghost of a monk?'

Mzz MacFarlane threw back her head and laughed uproariously.

'Maggi – what an imagination you've got! It was me, silly. I often sing to myself while I'm working up here – it stops me feeling lonely.'

Both the laugh and the lie were as real as a three-pound note. And Mzz MacFarlane's hand on the door jamb was trembling. And in the sunlight coming through the window of the room behind her, she was terribly pale.

Maggi couldn't bear it, she just ran away downstairs.

She lay in her sleeping bag on the old gilt couch, screwed up into a ball as tight as she could get. She didn't know what was worse, lying with her eyes shut, so she couldn't see if anything was creeping up on her; or lying with her eyes open, watching the blue moon-light from the uncurtained windows creeping across the old floorboards. Everything she looked at seemed changed by the moonlight; even her clothes on the one chair. Even Mr Abbot the bear, sitting in the corner, because there was nothing else to sit on. Even Mr Abbot who had been in this house for . . . how many years?

This house played tricks. It could whirl you back to 1953 with a bunch of dusty menus; or back to 1850, with a bleating goat; or back to a sniper who died in 1644 with nothing at all. And now back to the Middle

Ages and the monks, with a voice in a sunny garden. If she wasn't safe in the sun, how could she *ever* feel safe in the dark?

Like she'd been safe at home, at 17 Brannen Terrace – where a washing-machine was never anything more or less than a washing-machine. Where a bowl of peeled spuds remained a bowl of spuds till you turned them into chips.

She knew she only had to tell Dad she was *really* scared, and they'd be home by tomorrow night . . .

But Dad was happy; the twins were happy. Percy and Wolf were happy. Even Mzz MacFarlane was starting to make jokes. If she blabbed to Dad like a baby, she'd ruin everything for everybody. And as soon as she got home, she'd be fed up too. Because Doris Streeton would still be Doris Streeton . . .

There *had* to be another way.

Mzz MacFarlane knew what was going on in this house. Mzz MacFarlane had *heard* the singing, no matter how hard she pretended. If Mzz MacFarlane would only say what she knew, Maggi was sure Dad could sort it out. Well, Dad and Percy between them.

She would get Mzz MacFarlane alone, over the washing-up, tomorrow morning.

There was such comfort in that thought, she fell asleep.

Mr Abbot continued to stare his cross-eyed stare out of the moonlit window, across her huddled sleeping body.

CHAPTER 13

'Mzz MacFarlane, can I talk to you *alone*?'
'Of course. Will now do?' Mzz
MacFarlane settled herself at the table, hands folded
gently on the formica top. And was changed as if by
magic. A moment ago, finishing drying the dishes and
looking out of the window, she had looked dozy
and wide open to attack. But now, she looked every
inch the concerned headmistress, invincible. How did
grown-ups swing this kind of trick? And why had her
own voice, which she had meant to be firm, if not
mildly threatening, come out as a bleat for help? It
was infuriating.

She looked at Mzz MacFarlane's face, and knew
that it was hopeless. How could she insist that Mzz
MacFarlane had heard the voice, without calling her a
liar? Why was calling an adult a liar so unthinkable?
Children called each other liars; adults called each
other liars, like the politicians in Dad's *Daily
Telegraph*. But if she called Mzz MacFarlane a liar,
and Mzz MacFarlane told Dad . . . *wow*! World War
III!

'What *is* it, Maggi?' asked Mzz MacFarlane, all

sweetness and light. 'I'll help if I can . . .' Maggi couldn't think of anything to say at all.

It was Mzz MacFarlane's hair that gave her the idea; it was such a mess. It was obvious she washed it quite often; and ran a comb through it before meals, but the rest of the time it was a tangled mass that often hung in her eyes, so that her eyes peeped out like some animal in a bush.

'I don't know what to do with my hair, miss. To look nice.'

'I think it *does* look nice, in that ponytail. Very fresh and sensible.'

'And I don't know what to do about make-up, miss,' lied Maggi, outrageously. She never thought about make-up.

A great beaming glow descended on Mzz MacFarlane's face. The beam that said she thought she'd really *understood* something. 'Oh, Maggi, poor love, I do understand. You're growing up. And you haven't got a *mother* to talk to!' She stood up, inspired. 'Come to my room. I've got make-up and things *somewhere*. Mind you, they're as old as the hills.'

'I think you'd look nice in a Fergie-bow,' said Mzz MacFarlane. She stood, comb in hand, surveying Maggi's hair in the dressing-table mirror.

'I've got one,' said Maggi. 'I'll fetch it.'

When it was in place, it didn't seem to make any difference to her face at all. But suddenly, looking at Mzz MacFarlane's face above her own in the mirror, lost in its tangle of floppy hair, something made her say: 'What do you look like with a Fergie-bow, Mzz MacFarlane? You've got red hair—'

'Oh, nothing much, I expect.' Was the severe Mzz MacFarlane actually blushing a bit?

Some devil got into Maggi. 'Go on,' she said, holding it out. 'Try it!'

Mzz MacFarlane got busy with a comb, sweeping her hair back. Then put up her hands to fix the bow, and lowered them slowly.

The effect was incredible.

Mzz MacFarlane had the most beautiful ears Maggi had ever seen. Tiny, like little pink shells. And her jawline was smooth and clean, without a hint of sag. And her neck was long and slender and unlined. And her high cheekbones ... and her green eyes ... and her fine curving eyebrows.

Mzz MacFarlane, released from her bush of hair, was without doubt quite a stunner.

'Oh, Mzz MacFarlane, you're *lovely*! Why do you hide yourself under all that hair? I wish I looked like you!'

Mzz MacFarlane *was* blushing now. Looking

pleased and cross all at the same time. 'Never had time for that sort of thing . . .'

'Please keep on wearing it. It's a present from me. It'll keep your hair out of your eyes, when you're busy.'

'All right, if it'll please you,' said Mzz MacFarlane.

'And can we do lipsticks now, miss? I've never tried lipstick.'

Lipstick didn't suit Maggi at all; she wiped it off on her hankie as soon as she got back to the kitchen to make the morning coffee.

But it suited Mzz MacFarlane. She had a lovely mouth, wide but very clean-cut lips. She looked really sexy.

When Dad came in for his coffee, he was shattered. He just kept staring and staring at Mzz MacFarlane, when she wasn't looking. So did Percy. So did even Mr Timmins, who for once was quite silent on the topic of capitalist exploitation.

When she finally went out, back to her typing, Percy said, 'By gum, I never twigged she were a cracker like that . . .'

'Neither did I,' said Dad thoughtfully.

Mr Timmins still had nothing to say; though he looked rather sad and wistful for once.

And, oddly, Maggi's lies paid off in another way. After she'd washed up the coffee things, she met Mzz

126

MacFarlane, still with her hair back in the Fergie-bow, in the corridor. She smiled; Mzz MacFarlane smiled. They passed. Then Mzz MacFarlane suddenly called her back.

'Oh, Maggi . . . that voice you thought you heard . . . well, I have *thought* I've heard somebody singing . . . really ever since I got here. I thought it was just my fancies . . . with the wind . . . and it being the site of an old monastery. I'm afraid I told myself just not to be silly . . . but voice or no voice, I haven't come to any harm . . . even when I was here by myself. So . . . voice or no voice . . . it's harmless . . . not to worry, eh?'

And she was gone up the corridor.

After lunch, she was washing up when she thought she heard the voice again. She opened the kitchen door, panscrub in hand, to see where it was coming from. It seemed to be downstairs this time. And no longer idle and happy. But urgent, somehow, instead. Something made her follow it, without hesitation.

It seemed to be leading her towards the side door. She became aware of a scraping sound on stone, outside. Then something banged on stone, harder. And there was the distant sound of laughter, rather nasty laughter. She knew it was the job-creation lot. She wanted to turn back. But there was another sharp bang, and more nasty laughter. As if some living thing was being hurt.

She opened the door, and sunlight flooded in.

Six of the job-creation lot looked up from the terrace where they were working. Should be working. She knew they were supposed to be scraping lichen off the balustrade and garden steps, then coating them with some liquid that kept out water and frost damage. There was quite a lot of lichen lying loose on the gravel round their feet. But something was wrong. There were great lumps of broken sandstone amongst the loose lichen; their raw edges shone in the sun, with tiny myriad points of light, that told her the pieces had just been broken off.

And there was too much for it to have been some sort of accident. She looked at the silent watching boys. Five of them had scrapers . . .

Stuttwick held a hammer. Too late he tried to slide it under his denim jacket. Then he saw she'd seen it; and took it out again and laid it on the balustrade with a mocking smile. His eyes bulged a bit, and were the nasty green of gooseberries.

'Me hand slipped,' he said. 'It just slipped, honest.' He didn't even try to lie properly; he just didn't care. The others all giggled.

She glared at them all. Some dropped their eyes, a bit ashamed. But they were too many for her.

Soon they were all staring jeeringly at her again.

Stuttwick, emboldened by the giggles, picked up the hammer and knocked another piece of sandstone off the balustrade. 'See, you can't help it. It's rotten. The whole stupid house is rotten. It should be pulled down . . . made into a footer field . . .'

'I'm going to tell my dad.'

'She's going to tell her dad,' they all chorused, mockingly.

'Tell him,' said Stuttwick. 'See if I care. He can't do nuthin'.'

She realized with a prickle of fright that he was inches taller than Dad. Four of them were inches taller than Dad. Were they looking for trouble, laying a trap for Dad? Should she let it go?

Stuttwick raised his hammer, and knocked off another piece. More sniggers all round. She looked round desperately for Mr Timmins, who should be in charge of them. He was wandering about under the trees, well out of earshot. She wondered if that was deliberate.

Another piece of stone fell.

And then the boys' faces changed.

Dad's voice came from behind her.

'What's going on, then?'

There was a silence, an expectant silence, while he

took in the broken stone and the hammer in Stuttwick's hand.

'You little . . .' She could tell Dad was angrier than she'd ever seen him. As he stepped past her, she saw the hairs on the back of his neck were standing up like the hairs on the back of an angry cat. He stepped up to Stuttwick and held out his hand for the hammer.

Stuttwick didn't move.

Dad grabbed for the hammer.

Stuttwick moved his hand at the last moment, so Dad grabbed on empty air.

All the boys sniggered.

Dad grabbed again. Again Stuttwick evaded him. But Dad bumped into him, so he staggered slightly.

'Gerroff me,' screamed Stuttwick. Then he pushed Dad away with his free hand, so hard that Dad almost fell.

More, nastier, sniggers. The other boys gathered closer.

Dad made one swift movement. There was a nasty squelchy thud and the next second Maggi saw Stuttwick lying on the ground, with blood trickling down his chin.

Dad leaned over and picked up the fallen hammer.

At that moment, Mr Timmins came running up.

'You hit this boy!' he shouted to Dad. 'I *saw* you.

You used violence on this boy without provocation. I'm sending for the police . . .'

'Please do, Mr Timmins,' said an icy female voice behind Maggi. 'Good. I shall have a great deal to say to the police. I saw this boy hit Mr Adams first. So hard he almost knocked him down. Isn't Mr Adams allowed to defend himself against six hostile louts, four of whom are bigger than him? Perhaps you feel the odds were too heavily weighted in Mr Adams's favour?'

'I wasn't near enough to see,' said Timmins, sulkily.

'And why *weren't* you near enough to see, Mr Timmins? You are supposed, on the legal terms of my Manpower Services' contract, to supervise their work at all times. I have watched them knocking pieces off my property for the last twenty minutes, while you were no doubt admiring the insects in my grass. Do by all means summon the police, Mr Timmins. I want to lay a charge of criminal damage against this youth. And a charge of assaulting my site foreman. How will *that* go down with your superiors, Mr Timmins?'

'The lads were only having a bit of fun . . .'

'If that's their idea of fun, they'll never work on my house again.'

'You've signed a contract!'

'Which I am *itching* to tear up . . .'

'Oh, shut up, Timmins,' snarled Stuttwick. 'Can't

you see she's got you by the short-and-curlies? Who's goin' to believe us? The pigs always take the toffs' side . . .'

'And if I ever see you damaging my house again, I'll throw you off my property personally.' Mzz MacFarlane looked a bit like Boadicea.

'Let's go, Timmins,' said Stuttwick. 'It's Friday. We knock off early anyway.' The boys trailed off towards the mini-bus. But Timmins still stood his ground.

'These lads . . . you can't blame them . . . they've got no work, no hope, no prospects . . .'

'Why not try them in the demolition business?' said Mzz MacFarlane sweetly. 'I'd say they had *real* talent there . . .'

Timmins made an inarticulate noise, and stalked off.

Dad and Mzz MacFarlane turned and looked at each other.

'By, pet,' said Dad, 'you really saved my bacon there. Aah thowt I was headin' for the nick . . .'

'I thought you handled it rather well, Mr Adams.' Mzz MacFarlane was all lit up, with colour flaming in her cheeks.

'Aah thowt ye were against violence?'

'If you hadn't hit him, I would have. Look at my poor balustrade!'

'Aah can mend it, good as new.'

'Can you mend anything, Mr Adams?' She was teasing him, now.

'Anything but a broken heart, pet!'

Looking from one to the other, Maggi saw the sudden pain in Dad's eyes.

What surprised her was the sudden, echoing pain in Mzz MacFarlane's.

CHAPTER 14

Maggi's favourite bit of the day was after supper had been washed up. She and Dad went for a stroll, if it was fine, through the long narrow woods that lined the drive. The excuse was that they were collecting the twins for bed; for the twins had formed a passionate attachment to Percy, or at least Wolf, and Percy's motorbike; the first time they went to see Percy after supper, they didn't get back till near midnight.

But the stroll was much more than a shared chore. They were walking straight into the sunset, and Maggi found most Cheshire sunsets beautiful. Besides, the woods were full of living things, birds, squirrels, rabbits, even the occasional fox, and once a hare strayed through the boundary hedge from his favourite field. Maggi didn't know the names of half the things, and neither did Dad; Dad invented daft names for the birds, like 'tweeters', and 'bleepers', and 'great crested whatsits', and 'piebald thingummies'. He was happy, on those walks, and he kept Maggi in fits. Mam would've been pleased to see them ... Maggi had never been so happy in her life.

One evening, they passed Mzz MacFarlane's open

door, on their way out. She was still busy typing appeal letters. She looked up as they passed and said: 'Going for your walk?'

She pushed her reading specs up on her forehead, rubbed her eyes and looked so weary and sad that Maggi said, before she could think: 'Why don't you come with us? There's ever so much to see, this time of night.'

Mzz MacFarlane's face lit up so much, she looked beautiful again.

'If I won't be in the way . . .' Maggi was glad she'd asked her.

Till they got outside. Because if she and Dad knew nothing about birds Mzz MacFarlane certainly did. Everything that moved was named. Mzz MacFarlane explained in depth how you told a pied wagtail from a white wagtail, and how you told both from a grey wagtail, *and* a yellow wagtail. Mzz MacFarlane waxed lengthy on the territorial fights of robins . . .

Dad was so impressed he shut up like a clam; no jokes tonight. And Mzz MacFarlane made so much noise that she frightened away everything but a few rabbits. And then, in the absence of wildlife (on which she remarked frequently) she fell back on the problems of the Abbey's day. Dad began to look really fed up. Maggi was heartbroken; why had it all gone so *wrong*? Mzz MacFarlane could be such good fun when Maggi had her on her own. Why couldn't she be silly and fun with Dad there?

Maggi was still pondering on this, when she heard a noise among the rhododendrons to her left. Voices. Voices of boys. Boys on the rampage. It sounded like the job-creation lot at their worst. Except she'd seen them depart in their mini-bus three hours ago. Had they come back looking for some sort of trouble, or was this a different bunch of trespassers, vandals? She shot a sideways look at Dad, expecting him to go belting across there and sort them out, pronto. But Dad trudged on, listening to Mzz MacFarlane's endless lecture with his eyes miserably on the ground. He obviously hadn't noticed them. Was it just because he was so miserable?

There was a wild yell from the rhododendrons; and a crash of breaking branches. Nobody could've *failed* to have heard.

Dad went trudging on.

Another yell; another crash. To shame Dad into action, to *make* him take notice, Maggi ran across to the bushes herself. Plunging in among them, she soon found the track of the boys. A straggling path led through the bushes, floored with damp, frail and tender turf that had been really cut up by the boys' feet. Six sets of tracks; two pairs of Doc Martens, one much bigger than the other; three sets of trainers, all with different patterns on their soles, and a pair of old hobnails. And she had a nasty feeling the hobnails were Stuttwick . . .

She could still hear the boys blundering and smashing on, ahead. She followed cautiously, placing her feet as silently as she could. She would spot them, see who they were, then run back to Dad to report . . .

Raucous laughter, and a wild cheer just up ahead. She rounded the bend, and came across a sight that nearly made her weep.

A teddy bear. A teddy bear that, covered in mud, had been literally kicked to pieces. The body, split by the crushing of a muddy hobnailed boot, still had one arm hanging by a thread. The head had been thrown three or four yards further. The other arm was caught in a prickly bush, three feet off the ground, where it had been kicked. Looking around, she saw one leg lying in long grass.

The bear had been very like Mr Abbot; she thought for a horrible moment it *was* Mr Abbot; but this one had brown glass eyes, not yellow ones. But she was certain it had come from somewhere in the house.

Crying as much with rage as pain, she ran on after the boys. Another raucous triumphant shout made her run all the faster.

In a clearing among the bushes, she came upon a tree. And from the tree hung another legless bear.

Hung by a piece of rope round his neck. An old dart protruded from his plump stomach; an attempt had been made to set his body alight with matches. Both legs, wrenched off, lay below.

She was now beside herself; all thought of running back to Dad was forgotten. She just wanted to *smash* the people who had done this.

But where had they gone? She listened. There was no sound in the wood but the tweeting of birds. She looked for the tracks of their boots; but no tracks led off anywhere. She couldn't believe it; she looked harder, crouching close to the ground like Sherlock Holmes.

But no tracks, anywhere. And the turf was just as soft and tender here as anywhere else. They couldn't just have vanished into thin air. There was just a mass of tracks where they'd gathered round the hanged bear and . . .

Tracks leading back towards the house. Mingled with the tracks she'd been following. She hadn't noticed that before, in her hurry. The tracks came through the woods from the house, gathered in a circle, then went back the same way . . .

But that was impossible; they'd been ahead of her – at least their noise had. If they'd doubled back, they'd have run into her—

Unless—

Dad hadn't heard the noise they were making. Mzz MacFarlane hadn't heard it either, or she'd have gone and investigated.

Only she, Maggi, had heard it. As only she had seen the dying sniper, heard the voice in the garden.

Ghost noise; a noise from the past. It had happened again.

A little cool breeze, the first after a hot day, wandered through the bushes, making her go goosey all over.

But there was nothing to be afraid of. Only the sound of birds singing. Whatever it had been was quite gone.

And it wasn't really ghost noise, because it *had* been Stuttwick and his mates. It had been their voices; it was their footprints. They had come here, and destroyed the bears. She felt the hanging bear gently. It turned its innocent trusting face to her, heart-breakingly. But it was dry. It had not been hanging here overnight, because it had rained heavily overnight. It must have happened this lunch time . . . you couldn't have ghosts of living people, could you? She couldn't believe that Stuttwick and all his mates had suddenly died in the last three hours.

No, it was a . . . like a snapshot from the past. The house was telling her something again; telling her what had happened here this lunch time. Why? What did the house want her to *do*?

Save the bears, of course, stupid. The bears were part of the house. Goodness knows where Stuttwick had found them, but they must be part of the house. Save the bears!

She gently unfastened the rope round the neck of the hanging bear. Picked up his legs from the mud. Ran back towards the first bear.

She had quite a search for the last missing leg. But she found it in the end. Now her arms were full of bits of bear; she couldn't carry them all. She tried stuffing arms and legs in the pockets of her jeans; up the front of her T-shirt. Still she had too much to carry. And she was frightened the bits in her pockets would work their way out as she walked, and get really lost.

If only Dad was here to help. But he and Mzz MacFarlane must be at Percy's lodge by this time.

Then she heard voices, low voices. And heard Mzz MacFarlane laugh. A low relaxed jolly laugh. They'd waited for her. She ran through a gap in the bushes, nearly in tears again with relief.

And stopped at a truly amazing sight. Dad and Mzz MacFarlane were *playing*; like *kids*. There was a huge fallen beech trunk, and they were trying to walk along it, wobbling, waving their arms and laughing. Then Mzz MacFarlane nearly fell. And Dad put out a hand to save her. And she grabbed it. And still fell, dragging Dad down on top of her in a great heap.

They stayed there for a long minute, looking at each other. Then Dad suddenly jumped up and bent to drag Mzz MacFarlane up after him saying: 'You're worse than the twins. At *your* age!'

Mzz MacFarlane raised one lovely eyebrow. 'And what do you think my age is, sir?'

Dad looked embarrassed. 'Aah nivvor ask a lady her age . . .'

'Thirty-five next birthday,' said Mzz MacFarlane gaily, and laughed again. 'And how old are you, *old greybeard?*'

'Thirty-nine next birthday,' said Dad. 'Old enough to have more sense than climb trees like a kid.'

'So it *seems*, Mr Adams.'

'Call me George!'

'All right, *George!*' She said it like she was tempting him to do something. Perhaps, thought Maggi, climb the tree again . . . why was she panting so much? Was she *that* unfit?

'And what shall I call *you*, Mzz MacFarlane?'

'I thought you'd never ask . . . Catriona, if you please, sir!'

Dad took a deep breath. 'All right, *Catriona!*'

They just stood, staring at each other. For so long that now Maggi found herself not breathing. Something *awful* was going to happen. Something that might change the whole world. She couldn't bear it.

She ran forward out of the bushes, yelling.

Dad and Mzz MacFarlane jumped a yard apart, and looked as guilty as anything, as if they'd been caught *stealing*.

'What's happened?' asked Dad, looking at her burden. 'Punch-up at the teddy bears' picnic?'

Mzz MacFarlane laughed; that low glad laugh again.

Maggi burst into tears. She pretended the tears were all about the fate of the bears. But she admitted to herself that she was lying.

CHAPTER 15

Maggi was concentrating hard on sewing on the teddy bear's second leg, when she felt a light soft tap on her foot. Looking down, she saw its arm had fallen off again.

She threw the bear down in a rage; and watched with horror as the head came adrift, hanging on only by three long threads of cotton.

'Oh, *drat*!' she said. That was two evenings' work, bending nearly double, straining her eyes by the electric light, and all for *nothing*. The cloth was so old, and frayed so easily, and nothing seemed to fit back on properly.

Dad and Mzz MacFarlane looked up from where they were sitting.

'Give it up, love,' said Dad gently. 'There's some things past mendin'.'

She looked down at the face of the bear; it seemed to look back at her beseechingly. 'Dad, I *can't*. He *wants* to be mended; I can't just throw him in the dustbin.' She felt like crying.

Dad got up, and gathered the bits of bear together with his clever hands.

'It's too far gone,' he said. 'He's had his life. Let him go.' It was the voice he'd used to her when Mam died.

'No. NO-NO-NO-NO-NO!'

'I have an idea,' said Mzz MacFarlane tentatively. 'There are people who specialize in repairing old bears and toys. Doll's hospitals, they call themselves . . . let me ring round and see if I can find one.'

'And no doubt they'll charge the earth,' said Dad. 'It's just not worth it. Throwing good money after bad.' He was starting to get cross; he had a terror of wasting money.

Mzz MacFarlane looked at him steadily. 'It's my money, George. And I suppose, come to that, they're my bears, since they were found in the house.'

'Well it's your business, then! What a world – some folk can afford hospitals for dolls. Other folk can't get hospitals for themselves.'

But Mzz MacFarlane wasn't at all put out. 'And when they're mended, I shall give them to Maggi for her birthday.'

Dad glared at her; she looked back at him steadily; the way Mam used to, when they had rows, which they never had much. Maggi thought they were going to have a real row.

But Dad looked down first, gathering up his fags and matches. 'A fool and his money is soon parted,' he said. 'Aah'm off te bed.' But he'd lost the row, and he knew it.

After he was gone, there was a long silence. Then Maggi, miserable, said, 'Sorry I made that row. It was my fault.'

'Oh no, it wasn't,' said Mzz MacFarlane briskly. Maggi looked up, and saw she was smiling.

'He gets cross sometimes,' Maggi said. 'He's had a lot to put up with.'

'I know,' said Mzz MacFarlane. 'He's cross because he can't mend the bears for you.'

That was a new one on Maggi. But she knew it was right. How *could* Mzz MacFarlane understand Dad better than she could? She hardly knew him. All Maggi could think of to say was: 'The bears want to be mended. They want to go on ... they're Mr Abbot's family. All he's got.'

'Of course they do. And they shall.' Mzz MacFarlane gathered up the bits of both bears from the table. Suddenly Maggi had an irresistible urge to hug her.

Mzz MacFarlane hugged her back, for a long time. Then she detached herself, as if she was rather alarmed at having got herself into this and said: 'Men don't know everything. Even if they think they do.'

'No they don't,' said Maggi. Feeling so happy she could've burst, she fled from the room.

* * *

The next few evenings were oddly different; oddly cheerful. The weather had turned cold at night, as it sometimes does in the second half of August, and Dad got a fire going in the old kitchen range. Wolf and Percy got into the habit of calling after supper, and Wolf lay with his long nose pointing towards the flames, opening wary eyes for flying coals as the fire cracked and spattered. Percy shoved his old biking boots up on the brass fender, and told them the story of his life. It was fascinating; everything from shooting rats in his dad's barn with an air rifle, to the strange ways of the head hunters of Borneo. Even the twins stayed quiet to listen. Baz said Percy was better than the telly.

Sometimes, when they could get a word in edgeways, Dad or Mzz MacFarlane would tell a story about their foreign travels. But usually they were silent, listening, just exchanging glances when they thought nobody was looking, and pulling faces when Percy really told a whopper. Maggi had a strange feeling that though all the talk was coming from Percy, all the happiness was somehow coming from Dad and Mzz MacFarlane.

And yet sometimes there'd be another row. One night just after the twins had been sent to bed Mzz MacFarlane began going on about her time in Sri Lanka.

'It was so *happy*. The people are so *hospitable*. They didn't have much, but what they had, you were welcome to. If you called at a house, they wouldn't let you go . . . they made tea their special way . . . little things to eat . . . whole tribes, in and out of each other's houses. And so gentle and happy. I sometimes think we've missed the meaning of life in the West. We have all these consumer goods, but we don't *belong* to each other . . .'

'That kind of talk makes me sick,' said Dad suddenly.

'*What* kind of talk?' snapped Mzz MacFarlane.

'The wisdom of the Mystic East – the wicked ways o' the West. I don't think people should always be knockin' the country they were born in. Aah reckon there's good black people and awful black people – same as with white people. If they're so flippin' marvellous out East, why are we always having to send them food an' medical supplies? Haven't they got enough mystic wisdom to look after their own? Ye sound like that telly ad – "Sri Lanka, Paradise". They were still showing that long after them Tamil terrorists had started chopping little kids to bits and burning them alive in their houses . . .'

'Don't you *care* about the Third World?'

'Aah care more about the truth, hinny. Aah want Maggi here to know the truth. If she'd been a bit older, wi' a bit o' money of her own, she might have taken a holiday in Sri Lanka Paradise, and got blown up by a terrorist landmine . . . you're concerned wi' makin' the world how you'd like it to be. Aah've got to be concerned wi' the world as it is.'

'Oh, you're totally *horrible*,' shouted Mzz MacFarlane. 'You're a racist, like all white soldiers . . .' She burst into tears, and fled out of the room.

Dad looked terribly pale and guilty. He lit up a fag, and then stubbed it out just as suddenly, and went after her.

Percy looked up at Maggi, like a schoolboy who hears the headmaster coming.

'I'll be away, little missus. Got to get Wolf his supper, and frighten off them vandals.' And was swiftly gone.

Maggi sat on, staring at the flames of the once-happy fire. Dad did not come back. Mzz MacFarlane did not come back. They must be having a terrible row. Perhaps this would be the end of Cheshire. Perhaps they'd be going home tomorrow . . . after all, it was Mzz MacFarlane's money that was paying Dad's wages . . . she didn't know whether she wanted to go home or not. Dad and Mzz MacFarlane had got into some strange tangle she couldn't understand. But home was Doris Streeton . . .

She made up the fire to content herself; she made up the fire again; and still they didn't come back. When she could bear the waiting no more, she tiptoed out into the corridor; listened, and could hear nothing. She opened the door of the twins' room; they were both snoring, which made her feel even lonelier. She went back into the kitchen; the clock said twenty past eleven. And *every* night, *every*body was usually in bed by half past ten ... the minute hand moved as she watched, tilting down to half past eleven. And her world seemed to tilt with it. Like the *Titanic* tilting over further and further in that movie on the telly, and things breaking loose, and people starting to notice and to scream ... only it was she who was beginning to feel like screaming ...

She was not a nosy parker; she despised all nosy parkers ... she was terrified of what she might find. But she had to know what had happened to Dad. She'd look in his room first; he might have been so upset after the row with Mzz MacFarlane he'd gone straight to bed without saying goodnight.

She opened his door gingerly, terrified it would squeak and give her away. But the cold darkness inside, the total silence, told her he wasn't there, even before she saw his sleeping bag lying, in a track of moonlight from the window, as flat as a pancake.

She crept on past her own room; there was only

Mzz MacFarlane's room left, unless they'd gone outside to have their row, and the thought of searching for them outside made her heart fail . . . suppose they were lying somewhere in the woods injured . . .

Mzz MacFarlane's room was slightly open. Only silence came out. But she had to make sure. She poked her head round . . .

Two dark figures were in silhouette against the moonlit window. Sitting on the bed as still as statues, a long way apart. Only . . . both had a hand outstretched, and she thought in the darkness that their fingers just touched. She had a terrible fright, thinking perhaps they weren't Dad and Mzz MacFarlane at all, but ghosts. But then she could see Dad's beaky nose and moustache against the window. Then she wondered if they were dead; but Mzz MacFarlane gave a little sigh . . .

On and on they sat, staring at each other. It was so unnatural. Had the house *bewitched* them? Why were they sitting so still, just staring at each other? She didn't know whether to flee, or make some loud noise that would wake them from their trance.

She was just about to do something, when Dad sighed and said, 'Aah'll have to be goin', pet. God knows what the time is. What'll people think?'

'Do you always live by what people will think, George?' But Mzz MacFarlane said it sadly, not snidely. Dad got up; from the way he grunted and put his hands to his back, Maggi knew he'd been sitting there still a long, long, long time. What *had* they been doing, just sitting in the dark?

Still unable to guess, she fled silently, before one of them saw her.

CHAPTER 16

Breakfast next morning was the most silent meal they'd had since they'd come to the Abbey. Mzz MacFarlane looked very pale, and did no more than fiddle with her toast and marmalade. Dad buried himself in the *Daily Telegraph*. Even the twins sensed something was up, exchanged glances and got out without demanding seconds of toast.

It was the arrival of the mini-bus that broke it up. Dad swallowed down a whole mug of tea in great gulps and left without a word. Mzz MacFarlane murmured something about appeal letters and left straight afterwards. Maggi surveyed the wreck of the kitchen, with an awful cold feeling in her gut that somehow the world was coming to an end. Then she told herself not to be stupid, washed up and felt a bit better.

She came to a decision. In the face of adversity she'd bake a big steak-and-kidney pie for supper. The biggest ever. Dad's favourite; even the twins had no fault to find with it. It might even coax Mzz MacFarlane back into eating.

So she was absolutely infuriated, when she was

halfway through making it, and at the critical stage, to hear the voice singing upstairs. She was pretty fed up with the voice, and the other tricks the house had played on her. She'd *tried* to do what it wanted; and it always made trouble. And trouble was the last thing they all needed at the moment.

'Oh, shut up,' she said. 'Can't you see I'm busy?' If she left the pie now it would be *ruined*.

Still the voice persisted. And sounded urgent. But the devil was in her. She stuck her head out of the door and shouted: 'Shut up. Go away. I'm *sick* of you!' Then she remembered Mzz MacFarlane might be in her room, and might think she was going mad, shouting like that at nothing. But Mzz MacFarlane made no sign; she must have gone out too.

Maggi slapped the crust on the pie, and slammed it into the oven. At that moment, the doorbell, the old one, jangled above her head.

She looked up, wondering who could be ringing it; the front door was open. Must be some visitor . . .

It was not the main-door bell that was still swinging. It was another one, in the corner of the bell-board. A bell nobody had ever rung before. Not one Dad had ever mended. The little china label below it was so obscured by the brown kitchen grime of ages that she couldn't read it at all.

But as she looked the bell rang again. Urgently.

She got a chair to climb up on, to try to read the stained label. She still couldn't make it out. She climbed further, up onto the top of a cupboard, to reach it. As she got her nose next to it, the bell rang a third time. She rubbed the china label with a hand, then spat on her hanky; the grease on it was thick, and formed little black sausages as it rolled off under the impact of her frantic rubbing.

The label said GARDEN DOOR.

But that was impossible! The garden-door bell was the other one Dad had tried to mend. The garden door led out onto the terrace with the balustrade the job-creation boys had tried to smash. But Dad had had no success. Not only were the wires buried deep in the wall, but the very bell-handle by the garden door was missing, and the hole where it had been was cemented up.

The bell, black with verdigris, rang and shook again, just under her nose.

A bell with no handle to ring it.

'Oh no!' she said desperately. 'Oh no!' She scrambled down so scared she hurt her leg a bit.

The bell rang a fifth time.

'No!' she shouted at it. 'I'm not coming! I'm not coming!'

And then all the bells began to ring together. All ten of them, from the lost empty rooms. One after another.

She ran. She'd meant to make for the main door, to find Dad or Percy or anybody. But somehow she skidded into a load of old rubbish, hurt her knee and in her panic took the wrong turning. She was in the long dark corridor, and it seemed to be closing in on her, like a dusty tomb in which the light dwindled and dwindled. She became nearly mad to get outside, into light and air before the corridor closed up and suffocated her altogether. So when she arrived at the garden door, she didn't think; she just wrestled with the key in the lock to get it open. Especially as there was a clink of metal on stone outside that meant *somebody* would be there.

The door burst open. The first thing she noticed was that the gravel of the terrace was wet, from a sudden shower. The second thing she noticed was that it was littered with newly broken bits of sandstone . . .

Stuttwick. He looked up at her sideways, grinning, hammer in his hand.

'I knew you'd come, little sneak. Got sharp ears, aintcha? But who you goin' go run to now? They're all out in't woods, ain't they? Tough luck, little sneak!'

But for some reason, she was not afraid of him. By comparison with the power that had rung the bells, he was *nothing*.

'Ain't no good pretendin',' said Stuttwick. 'There ain't nobody home. I *watched*.'

She waited, silent. Not knowing what she was going to say; but knowing she was going to say something.

'I'm going to smash all this house up,' he said. 'Even after they've sacked me. I won't have anything else to do then, see. I'll just wait in't woods till you all go out then I'll *smash*. Till it ain't worth repairing. Then when you've all gone for good, I'll burn it down . . .'

She wondered why he should hate the house so much. She wished she could see inside his mind, but she couldn't. She could never understand why people vandalized, or scrawled graffiti, or stole the flowers off Mam's grave in the churchyard, then just left them broken and scattered. She was a maker, like Dad. Dad said makers and breakers would never understand each other . . .

Suddenly she said, 'It's *easy*, breaking the balustrade. Any fool could do that . . .'

'Yeah,' he said, 'great.' And knocked off another large bit.

'But you'll never get to *that*,' she said, pointing upwards to the great sandstone coat of arms over the door.

Having said it, she was aghast. She loved the coat of arms, with its beautiful supporting dragons, more than anything in the whole house.

He saw the sudden look of terror in her face, and laughed worse. Then turned to the corner of the porch, where great square stones stood out of the brickwork like vertical steps.

'Just see if I can't. Just watch me!' He began to climb, his hobnailed boots scraping bright weals in the blackened stone.

She just stood and watched him, paralysed. He reached the same height as the coat of arms, and began to work his way along a sandstone ledge towards it.

She couldn't even shout or scream; she couldn't even breathe. And then her eyes, following the soles of his boots as if they hypnotized her, saw a wide crack in the ledge he was working along. She saw his boot descend on the piece of ledge next to the crack.

The piece moved a little.

She knew the next piece was going to give way when he stepped on it. She was able to step back two yards, to take herself out of danger. But for some reason, she couldn't open her mouth to warn him.

He raised the hammer high above his head.

As it began to descend, the stone fell out of the ledge.

For a moment, fifteen feet up, he seemed to stand on nothing. Then his arms flew wide, as if he was trying to fly like a bird. His hands grasped, for things that were not there to be grasped. The hammer flew away over her head . . .

And then he hit the ground, with a terrible thud. And in the midst of the thud, there was a loud crack. No, three loud cracks, almost together. From inside his body. She hadn't realized you could hear bones crack *inside* a body.

Then he lay quite still. Only a little bit of wind ruffled his ginger hair where it lay bright on the dark wet stone steps. And the rain started to rain on him. And still he lay still.

She thought he was dead, till he moved his head. His face was so white, his freckles stood out like specks of blood. His gooseberry eyes had a sort of film over them, and he looked like he was watching something far away.

'Help . . . me,' he said. 'I can't move.'

She ran screaming for Dad.

It was late that night when she heard Mzz MacFarlane's Mini returning. Percy, dozing with Wolf over a roaring fire in the kitchen, never stirred. Wolf raised his head and huffed a bit, then put his head down again. It was not his business.

Maggi ran to the hall stairs, and sat down on the top step, out of sight behind the banisters.

The door opened, and Mzz MacFarlane stepped through. Then Dad, and closed the door behind him. They stood together on the great worn doormat; very close together. Mzz MacFarlane looked like she hadn't slept for a week; Dad's mouth was very tight, and he was chewing at his moustache.

'They say he'll never walk again,' said Mzz MacFarlane.

'They can work wonders, these days,' said Dad. But you could tell he was just saying it to cheer Mzz MacFarlane up.

'I blame myself,' said Mzz MacFarlane. 'If we'd never brought those boys here . . .'

'Don't talk so wet, woman. He was given permission to go to the toilet. He embarked on a deliberate piece of vandalism. He asked for trouble, an' he got it. He musta been mad, climbing up there. Aah wonder what drove him to it. Aah'll have to ask Maggi . . .'

Maggi trembled; she could never lie to Dad. But Mzz MacFarlane was in to her rescue like a flash. 'Don't, George, it'll only make her more upset, and she's upset enough already. It's enough to mark her for life.' Mzz MacFarlane put a slim hand on Dad's hairy bare arm. 'Leave it, please. For my sake.'

They looked at each other a long time. Then Dad lowered his head, and said, 'Aye, well, mebbe ye're right. Aah'd just like to be sure she hadn't provoked him into it, that's all.'

'George – it was you that provoked him. Knocking

him down in front of all his mates . . . What did you expect?'

'Aah divvent understand young lads any more. Aah wes young meself, twenty years ago – Aah wes no angel. But smashin' up good buildin's. Aah suddenly feel old, pet.'

'Not as old as I do. Old and bad luck. Ever since I came here.'

'Gerraway wi' yer bad luck – ye met me, didn't yer?'

'Oh, the arrogance . . .' But she smiled, wanly.

'Eeh, Aah could do wi' a good cup of tea. That hospital stuff . . .'

'I'll put the kettle on.' Mzz MacFarlane began to run up the stairs, her face hidden from Dad now oddly radiant.

Maggi just scrambled back to the kitchen in time.

CHAPTER 17

After breakfast, Maggi cornered the twins in the kitchen, alone. She hadn't slept a wink all night, and she didn't know *what* she looked like. But for once her looks were scaring the twins out of their wits . . .

'OK,' said Gaz, licking his lips. 'We'll do the washing-up. Pronto. *Promise.*'

'I'm not talking about doing the washing-up,' said Maggi. The words kept coming out of her mouth in a mixture of spit that was splattering the front of the twins' T-shirts. She kept stammering; her eyelids kept twitching. 'I'm talking about doing any damage to this house. *You will not do any damage to this house*, do you hear me? Not break one window, or kick one skirting-board, or steal anything nor even carve your names on anything. *Promise!*' She could hear her voice rising to a hysterical shriek.

The twins were staring at her, eyes so wide that she might have been the creature from the Black Lagoon. She was not only terrifying them; she was starting to terrify herself. She could see little reflections of her face bobbing about in their eyes. What could she look like?

Baz swallowed. 'Yeah, we promise. Can we go now?'

'You don't understand,' she yelled at him. 'Oh, you little fool, you don't understand. If you harm this house, it will *kill* you.'

'Hey, what the hell's goin' on here?' said Dad, poking his head round the door. 'Is it a private fight, or can anyone join in?'

Maggi glared at the twins, willing them to shut up. But she'd scared them too much; no honour among thieves this morning.

'Our Maggi's gone bananas,' said Baz.

'Right round the twist,' agreed Gaz. 'She says if we damage the house, it will *kill* us. Even if we just kick the skirting-board.'

'Tripe!' said Dad. 'Get out of here, the pair of you, afore I find you something to do. And if I hear any more talk of that sort, you lose a week's pocket money . . . Go on . . . GO!'

Then he swung on Maggi, his blue eyes blazing, as they hadn't blazed since he knocked Stuttwick down.

'What on earth you been telling them? I thowt at your age you'd have more flippin' sense. A big girl like you. Aah've been relying on you, te back me up wi' them. What *is* all this rubbish aboot the house?'

She knew it was hopeless, before she opened her mouth. He wouldn't listen; he wouldn't listen to one word in ten, and the words he did hear would only madden him more. But he would keep on and on at her, till she told him. And then he would punish her for telling him. Oh, he wouldn't hit her; she was a girl. No, he'd just look at her as if she was a *thing*; a smashed thing beyond hope of repairing. He'd try a long time, days, weeks, to repair something. But in the end, if he couldn't, he'd smash it with quite terrifying violence. Like he was wiping his failure out of existence. For days, now, he'd simply treat her like she didn't exist. And that she couldn't bear ... She wanted just to cry; but tears maddened him more.

Mzz MacFarlane sailed blithely right into the middle of the storm, saying, 'George, that money you wanted for the new guttering ...' and fumbling with her wallet. Then she stopped in mid-sentence, and picked up the atmosphere and said, shocked, 'George ...?'

The tidal wave of Dad's wrath nearly burst over her too. But Dad reined himself in like he was a rider on a panicking horse. The effort of reining himself in brought out sweat on his brow. It was a long time before he could speak. Then he muttered, 'Maggi's been spinning the twins some yarn.'

'What yarn?' Mzz MacFarlane turned to Maggi.

Maggi began spilling it all; because Mzz

MacFarlane's eyes were calm and kind. She started to mention hearing the voice singing.

But Mzz MacFarlane shook her head imperceptibly, warningly. So she stopped abruptly. Dad looked baffled.

'So . . . you heard Stuttwick singing,' said Mzz MacFarlane gently. Giving her a clue what to leave out; the bits that would madden Dad more. So she missed out the voice singing, and the bells ringing. When she'd finished, Dad said, 'So you knew he was goin' to fall?'

'Yes.'

'And ye did nowt to warn him?'

'No.' She added lamely. 'Something seemed to stop me . . . my mouth was all dry and I couldn't move my tongue . . .'

Dad gave that snort of disgust. But Mzz MacFarlane put a restraining hand on his hairy arm, and asked gently, 'You didn't think Stuttwick would hurt himself like he did?'

'I thought he'd sprain his ankle or something . . .'

Mzz MacFarlane turned to Dad. 'I think enough's been said, George?' There was a low but awful warning in her voice.

Dad shrugged. 'Aah divven't blame her; you know how Aah felt aboot that young lout. Mebbe she blames herself . . . but that's no call to put the blame on innocent bricks an' mortar . . . anyway, Aah've got work to do, if nobody else has . . . give us that money for the new guttering.'

Maggi closed her eyes in relief. His anger was over. She hoped Mzz MacFarlane would come back after she'd talked to Dad outside, so she could tell her the real truth.

But for some reason Mzz MacFarlane didn't come back.

Now, every morning, after breakfast was washed up, she warned the house. It became a ritual, when no one was about. She'd start in the ground-floor corridor, and walk every stair, every open space, right up to the attics in the roof. And in each place, after she opened each door, she looked round, then closed her eyes and said out loud in the silence, 'I know you're there. I tried to help you. I wanted to help you. I tried to mend the teddy bears. I tried to stop Stuttwick for you. And you made me nearly kill him . . .

'Just don't try to hurt the twins, that's all. Or Dad. Or Mzz MacFarlane. Because if you do, I'll burn you to the ground. I don't know how, but I will. And I don't care if you kill me. I'll still do it.'

There was never any reply. Perhaps the house listened; perhaps it didn't.

But there was only silence, and the smell of old

houses; the mushroom smell of dry rot, the acrid smell of damp plaster, mouse dirt and dust.

And that piece of wallpaper kept on falling off in the draught of the upstairs corridor; the piece of paper stuck over the beam that said the Roman numerals. In the end she brought up a tube of Dad's glue and stuck it back in place properly and finally.

And she found one more teddy bear, in a cupboard on the top corridor. A very small one. She wondered if the house was using it to say sorry. But she doubted it. Anyway, it wasn't enough to make up for Barry Stuttwick . . . Still, she called the small bear Charlie Abbot, and set him to sit next to his dad, Mr Abbot, in the corner of her room.

It was almost as if her threats had worked. Nothing odd or nasty happened for a week; nothing at all. It was very peaceful. With Stuttwick gone, the job-creation boys settled down, and worked hard. The rose garden was finally completely weeded. A very large number of potholes were filled up in the drive, and the piles of logs in the outhouses became a source of wonder to everyone; nobody would freeze for years to come. Percy cleared the chimneys of the great hall, by borrowing a shotgun from his brother-in-law, and firing it up them, bringing down mounds of soot, and the innumerable fine white skeletons of birds that had lived and died in the chimneys for about the last hundred years. They had roaring fires afterwards in the great hall, to dry it out, and sat in there for cocoa, listening to Percy's yarns.

Percy also took the twins fishing, which kept them away from the house. Only Dad was not content. He kept fretting about when he could get his hands on some *real* money. The slates should be re-hung before the equinoctial gales, or he would not be responsible . . . all the good work done so far would be undone. Mr German and Mzz MacFarlane talked vaguely about a meeting of the Marigold Trust Committee on the fifth of September . . . they would make the big decision. Dad snorted, and was rude about committees. He said a camel was a horse designed by a committee. But it was good-humoured snorting. He and Mzz MacFarlane went for the evening walks alone now. Leaving the twins in the charge of Maggi and Percy and Wolf. Maggi was content to let Dad go. He was happy. And she knew some woman would have got her claws into him sometime; he was too good a bargain to leave hanging around. Better a Mzz MacFarlane than a Doris Streeton. Though she couldn't imagine Mzz MacFarlane back in their little house on Tyneside; it would be like caging a bird. She belonged here. Perhaps they all belonged here. Perhaps Dad would become a Cheshire gentleman . . .

already, he spoke nicer than he used to. Mzz MacFarlane was rubbing off on him.

Maggi's dreams over the supper washing-up were rudely interrupted by the sight of the twins crouching at the edge of the lily pond that lay on this side of the rose garden. A long narrow pond, oblong in shape, with a sandstone edging all round. If it hadn't been for the lilies, it would've made a good swimming-pool. But the deep green lily-pads floated all over the surface of the water, leaving only a few shadowy gaps in which, if you were quiet, you could catch a sight of the one giant golden carp that still miraculously survived there. When she thought of it, Maggi kept a few bits of pie-crust or rice to feed him with. He seemed to like pie-crust best. Otherwise, she had no idea what he fed on.

There was something menacing, predatory in the way the twins were crouching there.

'Percy, what they doing?' she asked sharply.

'Fishing, likely,' said Percy, coming to look over her shoulder.

'For the *carp*?' She froze in horror. 'Mzz MacFarlane won't let them. She says it's over twenty years old.'

'They've nobbut a bent pin an' breadcrumbs and a hank of string,' said Percy. 'Tek more than that to catch a wily old carp. They're mekkin' so much noise it'll be at far end o't pool, well under cover.'

Half-reassured, she went back to the washing-up. But she was still uneasy. The twins were scattering breadcrumbs on the surface of the water now. The carp might think it was her with her pie-crust. And it *trusted* her. A sense of infinite wrong clouded her mind. She wiped her hands on her apron, hung it up and hurried off downstairs to break the twins' game up.

She was too late. As she approached the crouching backs, Baz gave a squeal of glee and shot upright, heaving with both hands. Incredibly the carp, all of eighteen inches long and a marvellous red-gold, and roundly fat came flying through the air over his shoulder, and landed, panting its gills, on the green turf of the surrounding lawn.

It all happened at once. Maggi screamed with rage at the twins; at the same time, as they turned to grab the carp, the carp gave a convulsive flap and squirm, and seemed to leap about a yard back towards the pool. Both twins grabbed for it together; their heads collided, and Baz went staggering back, stepped on nothing, and flailing, fell backwards into the lily-pond.

Screaming with laughter, Gaz forgot the carp, which gave another flap and wriggle in another direction, away from the pool. Maggi followed it, trying to grab it and put it back in the pond. Every second it was dying, suffering, drowning in air. She got her hands to it, but it slipped through, and fell back into the grass. As she followed it, bending, she heard Gaz's laughter turn to a frightened squeak.

'Baz, Baz! He's not come up. Maggi, where's Baz?'

She spun round. The surface of the water was convulsed with waves radiating from a spot about five feet from the bank. There was a hole in the lily-pads there, and the leaves were sticking up in all directions, like the bows of wrecked ships, and bobbing wildly. But of Baz there was no sign. As she looked, a tremendous mass of air-bubbles rose from the now-black water and burst on the surface, with a vile stink of death.

'Baz,' she screamed. 'BAZ!'

One small pale hand broke surface, grabbing at nothing, except the handfuls of green slime tangled round it. And vanished again, amidst more great convulsions of the black water.

'He's caught in the weeds!' yelled Gaz, starting a terrible sort of crying.

More huge air-bubbles broke surface. Baz's lungs must be empty now; full of black water.

Then his face broke surface. His eyes stared vertically upwards in total unbelieving terror. His mouth opened and closed, like the carp's had done, meaninglessly. Then he vanished again.

And a few more air-bubbles came up. But not many, now. He wasn't even moving about much down there, any more.

Maggi paused on the brink, and raised her hands to jump in after him.

But a mighty shove sent her staggering back to fall on the turf. As she looked up she saw Percy jump in instead.

The water did not come above his shoulders. But he ducked down into it. His huge hands rose above the surface, holding handfuls of long green weed. The weed had cut his hands; they were bleeding red streaks among the green. For ever the great hands rose and fell. And then, quite suddenly, Baz was between them. And then Percy's head appeared, and he came wading to the bank, carrying Baz before him; he threw Baz on to the bank, and hauled his own great body after him. Then he was bending over Baz, clearing the weed from his face, giving him the kiss of life.

He only stopped once, to shout, 'Ambulance, ambulance!'

Maggi ran.

When she got back, it was all over. Baz was leaning up on his elbows, coughing his head off and being sick on the turf. And Mzz MacFarlane and Dad had appeared out of nowhere. And Gaz was hunched up in a ball, sobbing as if his heart would break. And the carp was nowhere to be seen, alive or dead. Percy said he must have flopped his way back into the pond on his own.

CHAPTER 18

'Now look,' said Dad. 'Before you start! As far as I'm concerned, Baz and Gaz were messin' about with that carp from the pool, and they banged their heads together an' Baz fell in an' Percy dragged him out wi'out any bother at all, an' he's going to be all right. I ask you, does he *look* like anybody who's come to any harm?'

He pointed out of the kitchen window, to where Baz was climbing a distant horse-chestnut tree and bombarding Gaz with immature conkers as he tried to climb up after him.

'Boys will be boys,' said Dad. 'And accidents will happen. 'I *won't* have you gettin' hysterical about it. Now get on wi' peelin' the spuds, or whatever you're meant to be doin'.' He stalked away, his back stiff with anger.

Maggi stared after him. Again, she thought of a blinkered horse that could look to neither left nor right, but only see a little tunnel straight in front of its nose. Only horses didn't put on their own blinkers, like Dad did. Suddenly, he seemed a pitiable person; no more than a child. Pushing away anything that threatened his own happiness. But then he hadn't spent another sleepless night, interspersed with brief dreadful dreams of Baz's drowning face coated in green slime; dead already except for the trapped, terrified, staring eyes.

But at least *she* had it all worked out now. She knew why Baz was still alive; why Percy had been *allowed* to rescue him.

Because the carp had saved its own life by accidentally flopping back into the pond. At the last minute, the house had relented.

If the carp had died, Baz would have died. Because the house defended itself, and the carp was part of the house.

The house had a life of its own. It defended itself against all injury. It sucked people in to serve it, repair it, protect it. Like that great white shark on the telly that allowed those little fish to swim into its mouth to pick its teeth clean. Mzz MacFarlane, Dad, Percy, Wolf, were all the servants of the house; whether they knew it, like Mzz MacFarlane, or didn't, like Dad.

And at any time, if any of them did something the house didn't like . . . Even if Dad mended a window wrong, a ladder might give way and he might fall to his death.

She finished the potatoes as quickly as she could,

and got outside. She stood in the sunlit forecourt in a black rage, wishing she could burn the place down.

And eerily, found the means to hand.

The *QE2* was parked just by the front porch, with its rear doors open. Underneath it, slung on a special fitment Dad had made, was a thing called a jerry can. It was a big five-gallon petrol can, ex-army, that Dad used to keep petrol in, in case they ran out on a long journey. She knew that, with the rear doors open, it could be pulled out quite easily. It would be heavy, but not too heavy.

If the petrol was poured over the floor of the entrance hall, and then she threw a burning paper through the front door . . .

The old house would go up like a torch. The nearest fire-engine would be in Northwich, eight miles away. And if the house was on fire, no one would be able to get into the house to phone. The fire brigade would be half an hour getting here. And by that time the house would be alight from end to end . . .

It did not seem to be her own arm that pulled the jerry can out. Or carried its splashing weight to the steps.

Matches, newspaper? Dad always kept spare matches in the glove compartment. And there was an old copy of the *Daily Telegraph* on the driving-seat.

She was appalled by how easy it was all being. She

looked carefully round, to make sure everybody was a safe distance away.

The twins were still climbing their tree. The sound of Percy's saw came from the woods; Percy allowed no one to use it but himself. She heard, above the sound of the saw, Wolf barking.

It was Wednesday morning; the job-creation boys were not here.

Mzz MacFarlane had gone to Northwich shopping; the space where she parked her car was still empty.

Dad? Just at that moment, she saw him walk out of the woods to the foot of the horse-chestnut tree, and start telling the twins off.

All clear.

She bent, and unscrewed the ridged filler-cap of the can. She tipped it gently, and the strong smell of petrol came up to her nostrils, and the honey-coloured liquid began to spread over the floor of the entrance hall, running across the flat boards and vanishing down the cracks. The fumes made her cough; but she kept on.

Then a voice said, '*Don't*, Maggi.'

She pulled the can upright, and spun round; goose-pimples of guilt springing up all over her skin.

Mzz MacFarlane was standing there, with her car keys in her hand. And the Mini was parked in its usual place on the forecourt.

It seemed the worst kind of magic; why hadn't she

heard Mzz MacFarlane coming? How had the house got Mzz MacFarlane back just in time?

Mzz MacFarlane stepped forward, picked up the filler-cap and screwed it back in place. Then she lifted the can back into its place on the van, with a sinewy twist of her bare long arm. She closed the van doors, and then all that was left was a little patch of dark evil-smelling boards on the hall floor.

'Never try to do that again,' said Mzz MacFarlane. Her eyes were dark and empty as fag-burns in a blanket. 'A man tried that once. He'd lost all his money, trying to start a country club here. He was bankrupt, and tried to burn down the hall to get the insurance money.'

'What happened?' croaked Maggi, her throat suddenly dry as a desert.

'He spilled some petrol over himself without realizing. When he lit a match . . . he ran out on fire. The house never caught fire at all.'

'What *is* it?' whispered Maggi. 'What's it doing to us all?'

'I won't tell on you,' said Mzz MacFarlane, her eyes still as empty as holes. 'I'll take the blame for spilling the petrol. I'll say I was trying to get some to get a stain off my clothes.'

Then she was gone, away inside.

* * *

Maggi stayed on the forecourt. All feelings of guilt had quite departed. She was just *angry*. The house had *trapped* her. No wonder it had been so easy to get the petrol, papers, matches. The house had known Mzz MacFarlane wasn't far off. The house had *tempted* her; made a fool of her.

She glared at it, from a safe distance. How *dare* you? You're only bricks and mortar, and rotten floor-boards and a dicey roof. You're not as important as *people*.

Again, she saw Baz's drowning face . . .

And then she saw the house clearly.

All over, it showed traces of Dad's efforts. Where once broken drainpipes had let water trickle down the wall, there were now smart new drainpipes, painted black. Where there had once been broken windows, there was now new glass and new putty gleaming white. The forecourt had been cleared of the tall dead weeds, and regravelled by the job-creation boys.

But Dad had scarcely scratched the surface of the job. And already he'd been working here a month. And had spent two thousand pounds of Mzz MacFarlane's money, including his wages . . .

Of course, Mzz MacFarlane still had twenty-eight thousand left . . . but looking at the house and its decay, Maggi suddenly knew that thirty thousand pounds had *never* been enough. Of course, there was

Mzz MacFarlane's committee, who were going to be meeting to decide about the roof, on the fifth of September.

But where *was* this famous committee? Why did they never come and see what was being done in their name?

Suddenly, exultantly, Maggi was running for the woods and Dad.

Dad was mending a field gate, on the far side of the wood. Yesterday, it had sagged so much it wasn't worth trying to open. Now, with a new shining-white crossbar, it swung open and shut to the touch of Dad's little finger. His face was shining with pleasure.

Maggi paused. He looked so happy, like a child. Maggi felt like Judas. She knew all about Judas, from RE at school.

Judas betrayed with a kiss. Maggi betrayed with a smile.

'That's smashing, Dad. Wait till you get to that old roof on the house . . .'

Dad's face clouded over.

'Aah'll have to wait a long time, hinny. Fifth o' September . . .'

'Expect they have to be careful – that roof will cost a lot of money, won't it?'

'Near enough a quarter of a million, if you count in

settin' them big chimneys to rights. A job for one o' them big roofin' firms ... and *they* can't be summoned just by snappin' your fingers ...'

'But Dad –' she tried to sound dismayed, though her heart leapt with triumph – 'Mzz MacFarlane's only got thirty thousand – she told me. And you've spent some ...'

He just stood there, looking at her, hand on his lovely gate, as if frozen. He looked at her so fiercely his eyes seemed to go right through her. She knew she had done it now; she could never take it back. It couldn't be undone, like the petrol.

'How do you *know*?' he shouted, as if he was in pain.

But she only had to stand there, and repeat, 'She told me,' and know it wasn't even a lie.

He walked towards the house swiftly, swinging his shoulders and his arms, like a man looking for a fight. She followed, at a little distance.

She didn't have to eavesdrop; the row could be heard all over the house. Every so often, Dad's yells could be heard above Mzz MacFarlane's wild sobbing.

'Why didn't you tell me that was all you had?'

'Thirty thousand wouldn't re-roof a hen-coop!'

'Where *is* this famous committee of yours, then?'

And Mzz MacFarlane, shrilly.

'I had a committee but when they saw the house I'd bought, they all resigned. They said it was no good. But I knew it was *right* . . .'

'And what about all the fund-raising you've been doing?'

'I've got one or two promises . . .'

'You can't re-roof a house wi' *promises*.'

'George, you've got to have *faith* . . .'

A door slammed, violently. The sound of Mzz MacFarlane's sobbing continued.

Dad walked into the kitchen, and said, white-faced: 'You can start packin'. I've given in me notice. We leave Saturday, early. That woman must be *mad*!'

He walked out, and was gone for the rest of the day.

Maggi fed the twins, fended off their questions, and started her packing. Every time she started to feel guilty, she remembered Baz's drowning face.

CHAPTER 19

The next two days were the loneliest Maggi had ever known. Meals were eaten in an atmosphere like a silent thunderstorm. Dad did not come in for lunch at all; he worked all day with a desperate fury, as if he meant to leave no stone unturned before he went. He performed wonders; managed to force the lock that had for so long held the ceremonial iron gates closed; rebuilt the hole in the wall through which, all that month, they had driven the car and van. He made and lettered a new warning to trespassers and screwed it to the wall. But all his efforts were performed outside, in the brilliant sunshine that continued as if the whole world of the Abbey hadn't fallen apart.

Maggi took him out sandwiches, and a flask of tea, when it was clear he wasn't coming in for lunch. She thought it would be nice to sit on the grass with him, in the sunshine, and share his meal. But when he did consent to sit down for five minutes, he was silent and restless, tugging at the tufts of grass cruelly with his free hand, as if he really hated them. She looked sideways cautiously; his set face did not encourage her to speak. When she did try to ask him about things, like should she write to old Mr Sanders, to get him to order some milk for Saturday, back home, he just snapped things like: 'You're running this family. Do what you like.'

Mzz MacFarlane at least kept her manners. But she often had to be spoken to three or four times before she would answer. She seemed to be in a permanent daze. And she stayed inside the house, as Dad stayed outside. She was very pale and sad; but at least she still spoke to Maggi like she was a human being.

The twins were awful. They hated the idea of going home, and took it out on Maggi at every opportunity. They said the washing-up wasn't worth doing, since they were leaving. They refused to give up their clothes for washing, till they were black with grime. They raced around the house and grounds, shouting like banshees.

But at least the house did nothing. Maggi watched and waited, through the long hours of the day, and the longer sleepless hours of the night. She felt ready to drop; it was only the thought of going home that kept her going. She would lift her head from the endless chores and think, 'In forty-eight hours we'll be on the road.' Slowly it became thirty-six, then twenty-four. And still the house did nothing.

And then, on the last evening, things seemed to take a

turn for the better. Dad said he would take the twins to the pictures in Northwich, to reward them for a summer of, for them, remarkably good behaviour. He asked Maggi along too. But she took one look at Mzz MacFarlane's forlorn face, and said she'd rather stay at home on the last night.

Dad read her like a book. All his irresistible charm came back; Mzz MacFarlane must come too; and eat chips coming home like one of the family. With the pale ghost of her former smile, Mzz MacFarlane listlessly agreed. Maggi stacked the supper things unwashed, in a hurry, and they all bundled out to the QE2. For once, the twins didn't mind going in the back. Maggi sat astride the gear-lever, half on Dad's seat, and half on Mzz MacFarlane's. It felt strange, but safe, to be bumping hips with two such different people at once. Dad's hip was old, familiar, comfy. Mzz MacFarlane's hip was softer, gentler, politer even in the bumping as they belted up the drive.

As they paused in the entrance, waiting for a car to pass, Dad glanced up at clouds in a sky already darkening.

'Mare's tails! There's a right wind comin'!' Long ago, Dad had loved predicting the weather; but since Mam had died, he hadn't cared whether it snowed or blowed.

The wind was already with them. It caught

them as they crossed the flyover across the A556.

'We'll get there in time, anyway,' said Dad. 'This old bus can do fifty-five wi' a gale behind her. Nearly as fast as the *Cutty Sark*!'

Maggi wondered darkly why he was so suddenly happy. Was it just the end of a job well done, or was it the prospect of getting back to Mrs Streeton?

They had the lot in the cinema. Sweets each to go in with, and ice creams in the interval. The twins crackled their sweets and giggled; but not enough to make the people round them actually grumble. Dad and Mzz MacFarlane, sitting one at either end, had plenty to say to everybody except each other. The film, a re-run of *Ghostbusters*, seemed pretty stupid to Maggi, now she'd had her own ghost. But it was nice pretending to be a family again, with Mzz MacFarlane there, instead of sitting alone in her old Abbey.

She'd be alone tomorrow night . . .

And how many nights after that? Suddenly Maggi was *desperately* worried for her; what was her life going to be, except endlessly wandering around those terrible dark corridors? Maggi wanted to turn to Dad and say: 'Let's take her home with us. We'll manage *somehow*!'

But she knew it was impossible even to *say* it.

They came out at ten; and the wind nearly knocked them off the cinema steps. In fact Mzz MacFarlane would have fallen, except Dad put an arm round her to steady her.

The two of them clung together for a bit longer than strictly necessary; they stared at each other, and even in the dim light, Maggi could see their faces reflected each other's pain. She felt terrible. But the vision of Baz's drowning face came to her rescue, blotting their faces out.

As they waited for their chips in the Seafarer, the whirling sign outside made a sinister buzzing sound, it was whirling around so fast. And the big fibreglass figure of a fisherman in yellow oilskins, holding up a huge silver cod for the public's approval, was rocking on its heavy base so badly that the manager went outside and fetched it in, where it made a looming presence, bigger than a man, at the back of the queue for chips.

The journey back was both wild and cosy. Wild with whole sheets of water beating against the windscreen and almost stopping the wipers; wild with the van's headlights swaying around the flooding black road, as the wind rocked them. But inside it was dim and warm, with her body between two big kind bodies, and the smell of chips. It was pleasant to look outside, and worry if they were going to make it; then look inside, and see Dad's strong steady face and hands on the wheel, and know they *were* going to make it.

They nearly didn't. The Abbey drive was littered with twigs and leaves broken from the old beech trees. Then whole branches, their wounded jagged ends white and ghostly in the headlights. And then, on the halfway corner . . . the biggest beech tree of all . . . it seemed to be swaying an awful lot . . . one way . . .

'Dad, it's *moving* . . .'

But Dad had already seen it, and clapped on the anchors, and was putting the van quickly into reverse. And they just sat and watched in horror as the great roots sprang up suddenly from the earth like black giant's arms, and splits ran along the black like white lightning flashes, and the noble old giant still struggled to get back upright whenever the gusts eased, as if it were fighting for its life. But the wind would not stop, and in the end it fell in a horribly tangled ruin of jagged ends of branches, and the pale undersides of leaves that would never lie smooth and straight again.

'Eeh,' Dad said, 'I'm sorry to see that go, pet!'

'It's all right,' said Mzz MacFarlane in a low voice. 'We'll plant some more, one day.' But her lips were pressed together tightly, and, wonder of wonders, she accepted a fag from Dad when he offered her one.

They got the van past the tree, with a lot of backing and slipping. Dad parked it round the far side of the house, where it wouldn't be blown over on its side.

They made it back to the entrance, clinging together to stay on their feet. Inside Dad pressed the light-switch. Nothing but darkness.

'Power's gone again. Maybe the main power line's down, between here an' the road. Ah'll check the fuses but . . .'

'I can brew up on my camping stove,' said Mzz MacFarlane.

'Supper-drinks,' said Dad.

Maggi thought that was funny. 'Brew-up' was Dad's word. 'Supper-drinks' was Mzz MacFarlane's. Why were they always exchanging words?

They edged forward by the light of Dad's lantern. They were halfway up the stairs, when Dad said: 'What's that jangling? The wind's knocked something loose.'

But Maggi knew, with a sinking feeling in her stomach, that the wind had not blown anything loose.

The jangling was the servants' bells on the board high up on the kitchen wall. The house was summoning them. Even in her terror, it gave her a certain grim satisfaction. She would say nothing; she didn't have to say anything.

Let Dad find out for himself.

Ahead of her, the jangling stopped again. They reached the kitchen door in silence; Dad opened it, and still it was silent.

Then, loud enough to make you scream, all the bells on the wall jangled together at once.

Everybody jumped. Dad smothered an oath. She saw the beam of the lantern swing up to the corner; and saw all the bells were still vibrating on their black coiled springs.

As the torch-light rested on them, they jangled again. This time along the row, one after another, very slowly and deliberately, as if the house was taking its time and making its point.

But Dad would still not believe.

'It's the flippin' wind,' he said. 'Amazin' what wind can do, in an old house.'

The bells jangled again, one after another, in a row. Only this time they rang slowly and deliberately in the opposite direction.

'I'm not having *that*!' said Dad in a low angry voice. 'I'm not having those ringing all night. We won't get a wink of sleep. I'll wedge them wi' paper.'

He grabbed an old newspaper, and folded it rapidly with his clever hands into thick wads. Then he leapt up on the cupboard, and slammed in the paper wedges between the bells and the wall. The awful thing was, the bells rang out while he was doing it, until the wedges silenced them. He looked like he was fighting an animal up there; strangling it with his bare hands. Maggi could hear him panting, like he was in a fight. 'Aah'll settle the beggar's hash!'

And at last the bells were silenced.

In the dim light of the lantern, Maggi looked at Mzz MacFarlane, and Mzz MacFarlane looked at Maggi. They both knew he was wasting his time.

And then the voices started. Not one voice only, but two, three, four. One deep and low; two high and shrill; one with a strange nasal intonation. Far off; in different parts of the house. Rising and falling; weaving in and out of the sounds of the gale. Maggi heard them; one glance at Mzz MacFarlane told her she had heard them too. Then the twins began exchanging baffled, wondering looks.

Only Dad did not seem to hear them.

'Aren't we going to have a brew-up?' he said, with untypical sharpness.

Mzz MacFarlane filled the kettle, and lit the camping stove. But from the way she stood, you could tell she wasn't expecting she would get the chance to actually make some tea.

Through the sounds of the gale, the sounds of the voices drew nearer. Baz and Gaz slowly edged next to each other, as they always did when they were expecting trouble. Dad went and stared out at the rain lashing the night-darkened window. He lit a cigarette, and Maggi saw, for a moment, his lit-up face reflected in the glass; only you couldn't read its expression.

Except – he looked like a soldier – one of those grim bronze soldier's faces off a war memorial.

Then Baz said abruptly, tightly, 'Hey, Dad, there's fellers singing, outside.'

'Just the wind,' said Dad, equally tightly. 'Wind plays some funny tricks in an old house. Specially a gale like tonight's.' And he began to tell some long and rambling story about working in an old house when he was a young man.

But nobody was listening. And the voices began to win over the noise of the gale. They seemed in the corridor outside. They seemed at the very door ... You could make out words.

'Daisy Ray?' whispered Maggi.

'*Dies Irae*,' said Mzz MacFarlane, flatly. 'It's Latin – it means "Day of Wrath". It's rather a dreadful ...' Then, like a sleepwalker, she began to move towards the door.

'Don't go *out* there,' snapped Dad, suddenly whirling round from the window.

'If it's just the sound of the wind,' said Mzz MacFarlane, 'why shouldn't I go out there?'

Dad had no answer.

'They want us to do something,' said Mzz MacFarlane. 'They want us to follow. They do no harm, if they get what they want ...'

And indeed, by the time she put her hand on the

door-handle, the voices were already fading along the corridor.

She went out into the dark. With a strangled curse, Dad followed her with his lantern. Maggi thought he was quite unafraid; only terribly angry, outraged.

Maggi followed him. 'It's all right, Dad,' she whispered. 'They don't mean no harm, if you do what they want.'

'Why should they be allowed to trouble the world?' said Dad bitterly. 'There was never a trace of your mam . . .'

The voices had drifted upstairs. They followed in single file, Baz and Gaz tagging on at the back, very close to Maggi, so they bumped into her every time Mzz MacFarlane paused. They climbed the narrow stair to the top floor.

And suddenly the voices ceased. Just the wind remained.

And with the wind, a little grating noise, overhead. A stony noise; stone grating on stone. Dad's torch-beam flicked up. All it revealed was a sagging plaster ceiling, and something small dropping. Something that left a dark stain on the bare floorboards. The grating noise increased as the sound of the gale increased; lessened as the sound of the gale lessened. Dad gave a cry of understanding, in which relief and fear were oddly mixed. Maggi knew that Dad was back in a world he understood. She also knew the news from that world was bad.

'The roof-slates is shiftin'.' said Dad. 'The gale's shiftin' the roof-slates.'

CHAPTER 20

Dad ran for the little wooden staircase at the end of the corridor. It led up to a hatchway that led out onto the roof. He fought with the rusty bolt that opened the hatch, as they all piled up behind him on the stairs.

He got the bolt loose. The wind blew in the hatch door with a force that sent him staggering back, nearly knocking them all downstairs. The wind swept into the house, sending their hair streaming out behind them, making them cling onto the handrail for dear life and filling their eyes with tears. It did seem to have stopped raining, though the odd spot of water hit their faces and chests with the force of a bullet.

'You see, it's useless,' said Dad hopelessly. Maggi wiped the tears from her eyes, and poked her head over the hatch rim. In the light of the lantern, which Dad struggled with both hands to keep steady, she could see the great slates just below the chimney stack. With every gust they were lifting and falling, like the jaws of flat grey crocodiles; like the leaves of a book.

'It's the windward end,' said Dad. 'If they start strippin' off there, it'll not stop till there isn't a slate left. You'll have no roof by mornin'. And all the slates broken on the ground. And the rain'll be right through the house. It's hopeless . . .'

'Hopeless be damned,' screamed Mzz MacFarlane against the sound of the gale. 'More weight would hold them down.'

'We haven't got weight . . .'

'*I* have!' screamed Mzz MacFarlane. And in another second she was out of the hatch and crawling across the wet sloping roof like a great big pink-tracksuited spider.

'She's mad,' whispered Dad. 'She'll be killed for sure.'

Mzz MacFarlane's voice came back to them, like a defiant windblown rag: 'This house is *my* responsibility!'

As they watched aghast, she reached the moving slates. She spread herself across them, at the very edge of the roof. She had found some sort of rod, an old lightning conductor running down the corner of the chimney, and was clinging to it with both pale slender hands, for dear life, as the next great gust came.

The slates moved a little, but only a little, and her body moved with them.

'See?' Her defiant shout came back to them.

'Daddy, it's *working*. She's *right*!'

'Aye – till she's soaked an' her hands go numb . . . she'll not last half an hour.'

'*Help* her.'

'What – an' put you in a bliddy orphanage?' Dad's voice was not at all afraid. Just *torn*, that was all.

'*Help* her.'

Dad crawled away, out of the hatch and across the black shining roof. He was much quicker than Mzz MacFarlane. Much better at it. The two of them huddled together by the chimney stack. Maggi listened hard, but the gale snatched away what they were saying to each other.

Then, after an age, Dad was crawling back. Alone. Halfway back, on the open slates, the gale caught him; he lost his grip and began to roll, over and over, helplessly.

The only thing that saved him was that the wind blew him back into the mouth of the hatch. Maggi heard his breath come out in a great whoosh of pain, as he hit the edge. Then he was tumbling inside with her.

'She'll not come back,' he gritted, through pain-clenched teeth. 'Not unless Aah knock her unconscious. Then Aah couldn't manage her across the roof. She'll not come back unless Aah mend the roof . . .'

'Can't you try?'

He looked at her strangely. 'If that's what you want . . . all right, then. Baz, Gaz, come wi' me. Aah need some stuff . . .' He gave Maggi the lantern. 'Keep shinin' the light on the chimney, so she can see what she's doin'.'

Then they were gone from her side. She held the light as steadily as she could, bracing it against the bottom of the hatch; though it still wavered as the wind hit her. It began to rain again. Mzz MacFarlane just went on lying there; her pink tracksuit getting wetter and wetter till it shone dark as a seal's pelt and clung so close to Mzz MacFarlane's body that she looked almost naked. Her red hair blew free of its black ribbon and flogged around the wet slates like the flag of a beaten army. Her face was set towards the gale, and invisible; there was no way of telling if she was alive or dead, except her pale hands were still clenched round the lightning conductor. Maggi shouted to her twice; but there was no reply.

Then Dad was back, with a rope round his shoulder, and a canvas satchel which had the handle of his heaviest hammer sticking out of it. The satchel clinked heavily; she knew it was six-inch nails, the biggest weapon in Dad's armoury. Then the twins were passing up other tools and ropes. And Dad was crawling out into the black maelstrom of wind again.

Now time was a whirl of terror. Now she knew the difference.

If Mzz MacFarlane died, it would be very sad.

If Dad died, it would be the end of the world. And she had sent him out there.

She held the light steady as he reached the chimney again. As, gauging the lulls in the wind, he raised himself to his knees above Mzz MacFarlane's body, on the very edge of the roof, and raised his hammer. As if he meant to murder her, to dash her brains out, or nail her to the roof, to crucify her. And the first six-inch nails were driven in, that would hold the slates in place till morning.

Then another gust would come, and he would crouch on top of her, two more hands clinging to the lightning conductor on the chimney, till the gust passed.

Was that rain on his hands? Or blood? Surely rain couldn't be that dark? Blood on his face?

And at last she heard Dad shouting to Mzz MacFarlane. 'It's all right, Catriona. It'll hold now! It'll hold, I tell you.' And she saw his bloody hands prising her pale hands from the lightning conductor, finger by pale finger. And then he was crawling back towards the hatch, dragging her limp body beneath him.

And then, as his hand was groping out toward the

very edge of the hatch, a great gust caught them, and whirled them away down the roof; and as her lantern-beam followed them, they rolled over and over and off the edge of the roof and out of sight.

CHAPTER 21

She waited, eyes screwed up, to hear the terrible thud as they hit the ground; a thud like Stuttwick had made, with breaking bones inside it; only worse.

For some reason, it didn't come. Perhaps the wind had carried the sound away; and yet she felt she would have *felt* it, as well as heard it.

Without allowing herself any hope at all, she shone her lantern down the roof again, where they had vanished.

Nothing. Nothing for more heartbeats than she cared to count.

And then something pale, fluttering, A rag, a rag borne on the wind? No! It moved against the direction of the wind. And it had four fingers and a thumb. She had a terrible vision of Dad dead and broken, and the terrible wind still blowing his arm around, with the pale hand on the end of it, like a flag.

But the hand gestured, beckoned. Like a ghost's hand, but more urgent, though awfully slow and feeble.

And a sound, a rag of voice, but Dad's. She thought the word it said was: 'Rope!'

It was enough to break the spell; to shove her into action. The stillness of death drained out of her, and the frantic desperation flooded in.

'Hey, Gaz! You!' She seized his paralysed shoulders and shook him.

'Go and phone. Fire brigade. Dial 999. Go on, stupid. GO ON!'

Saucer-eyed, white and trembling, he stared at her; so she had to shout the same thing at him, over and over. Till finally he was no longer between her battering hands, but running down the stairs in the dark. She turned to the other one. 'Baz – the rope!'

He was quicker on the uptake. The rough thickness of the rope was suddenly in her hand.

'You gotta put it round somethin',' he gasped. 'So it'll *hold*.'

By the shaking light of the torch, they searched for the strongest thing to put it round. The strongest thing seemed to be the square rough post that held up the little wooden stair. She wanted something far, far thicker; but there wasn't anything . . .

Baz put the rope round the post, and gave it to her. She tried to tie it round her waist.

'Not like that, stupid,' he shouted. 'That's a stupid granny-knot. Here . . .'

She let him; he was good with knots; he'd been a Wolf-cub, and was thinking of joining the Scouts.

He tied it good and tight around her waist.

'When you want more rope, tug on it,' he shouted. And helped her to climb out of the hatch onto the roof. Immediately a great gust came, and picked her up, and blew her away. Except the rope cut hard into her waist, making her cry out, and she just banged against the side of the hatch instead. She opened her mouth to yell, and the gale stole all her breath away.

Then the gust died; she tugged on the rope and felt herself slide down the rough slates. Kept on tugging and sliding, down into the blackness. Looking back, she could see only the edge of the hatch, outlined by the light of the lantern.

Halfway down, another gust lifted her into the air, and threw her hard to one side. The rope was cutting her in half; what with the wind and the rope she couldn't breathe; she was choking to death. And then the gust went away; and she slid on, sideways and down; no more use than the lead weight on a fisherman's line. How could she do anything to help, supposing she ever got there? It was all blackness and wind and hopelessness.

And then a hand grabbed her ankle; and from its strength, she knew it was Dad's hand. He pulled her close. The gale suddenly dropped completely.

She looked down. A dim view of the forecourt; with Mzz MacFarlane's Mini parked, looking no bigger than a Dinky toy. And, nearer, what Dad and Mzz MacFarlane had fallen on; the shallow sloping roof over one of the bay windows that went from top to bottom of the house front. A sloping roof with a little bit of crenellation round it, like a miniature castle. That was all that had stopped their fall. Mzz MacFarlane lay wedged between it and the sloping roof; and Dad lay on top of her. Her head seemed to be back, and her eyes shut . . .

'She's alive,' said Dad. 'But she's hurt.'

As he spoke, she moaned and stirred. At her movement, there was a grating of moving stonework.

'What's *that*?' The sound terrified Maggi.

'Stonework's rotten,' said Dad. 'It's all that's holding us, and it's *moving*.'

'What do I do?' she gasped.

'Can you climb up the rope wi'out bein' tied on it, pet? Get back to the hatch on your own? I need the rope to tie round Mzz MacFarlane . . .'

She looked at the climb back up the slates to the hatch. It didn't look very far. Not as far as when you climbed the rope in the gym at school, to the gym ceiling. And that was vertical.

The stonework beneath Mzz MacFarlane grated and moved again.

'OK,' said Maggi.

'Keep a good grip on the rope,' said Dad. Then she

felt him undo the rope from round her waist. They waited for a calm patch in the wind, then: 'Off you gan, pet.'

She went up it hand over hand, like a little monkey, like a whirlwind. But it wasn't like the gym. The rope was too thin; and soaking wet and slippery. The slates were wet and slippery and stubbed her toes. She felt so *tired*, like an old woman; her arms ached so; she wanted to let go, but if she once let go . . . terror drove her on, like a blind flailing machine.

She was nearly up to the hatch; within hands-grasp of it, when the next big gust hit her; threw her sideways. She nearly lost her grip. She fell and skidded so she didn't know if she was sideways on or upside down. I'm going, she thought, I'm going. Her hands began opening of their own accord, the rope began to slip upwards through them.

And then it felt as if a great warm arm picked her up and threw her back to the hatch. She banged into it, felt an edge, tried to grab. Baz grabbed her instead and pulled her inside roughly and painfully, like she was a sack of rubbish; and she thumped down on the stairs. She couldn't believe she was there, safe.

'What . . . what . . . threw me back?' she gasped.

'The wind, o'course. Coming the other way round the roof,' said Baz. 'I *saw* it.'

'How can you *see* wind?' she gasped, scornfully. But

she supposed he was right; she'd been saved by a fluke, a lucky fluke. Only it had felt like a big warm arm . . .

'Rope's gone tight,' said Baz. 'Dad must've tied it on. Take the end; he'll be an enormous weight; I can't lift him on me own.'

But there was no more movement on the rope. So they settled, tense, holding it tight.

'Where on earth is that wazzock Gaz?' said Baz. 'Where the hell *is* he? An' the police? An' the fire brigade?'

But in the end, it was a single headlight that came to their rescue, bumping up the drive through the storm. The frantic chugging of Percy's motorbike, and the low barking of Wolf. Still, it sounded as good as the Seventh Cavalry bugle in a Western.

Five minutes later, Gaz slid in beside them and took his share of the rope.

'I dialled 999,' he said, 'but the silly twit wouldn't believe me, 'cos I was a kid. Percy's giving her hell now.'

Percy dropped down another rope for Dad; firmly tied onto a main beam in the corridor below. Which was just as well. It was an hour before the fire brigade got there.

CHAPTER 22

They didn't leave the following morning. They all sat around in the kitchen. Maggi made endless cups of coffee till the milk ran out. The males told their stories over and over. Gaz's run through the falling trees of the drive, every one of which seemed to have missed him by inches. Baz's amazing snatch of Maggi from certain death on the roof. What Percy had said to the fire brigade, and what they had said to him. Only Dad was silent; he kept staring at quite ordinary things, like the table or the washing-up bowl, as if he was just glad they were there. When the rest finally shut up, he said abruptly, 'Maggi was very brave.'

She blushed, and shook her head, and plunged back to the washing up. What else could she have done? It was *Dad*, out there in the dark and danger. It would have been much harder, impossible, to just leave him there.

In the afternoon, they went to collect Mzz MacFarlane from hospital. She had one arm in a sling; she looked pale but quite beautiful; very calm and smiling. Maggi got five more pints of milk from the village shop, on the way home.

She was peeling another lot of potatoes at the kitchen sink, when something tiny dropped on her head. She might have thought it was a bit of plaster, or a spider, except it wriggled down through her hair and felt icy-cold on her scalp.

A drop of water. She looked up at the kitchen ceiling, and another drop of water hit her in the eye. Squinting up again, she saw another drop slowly growing.

Funny! She knew there was no water-tank or pipe at that particular point that might be leaking. And it had long since stopped raining; it was a calm sunny day again, outside, the dark greens of late summer freshened up by the night's storm. She almost didn't go and check; she felt tired and pleasantly lazy, now everybody was home safe.

But another drop of water hit her on the head. So she dried her hands and went up to look. It wasn't serious enough to bother Dad with, while he was having a well-earned kip. Mzz MacFarlane was resting too, on doctor's orders, and Percy had taken the twins fishing; though she betted there was more boasting than fishing going on . . . She wasn't expecting anything really; the house felt empty, lazy, asleep, as if it too was weary after the wild night.

The top corridor was a shambles; especially the far end where the slates had nearly come off the roof. The ceiling had collapsed in great drooping wet sheets of plaster. Dad might have made certain, first thing this morning, that the slates of the roof were still in place; but a lot of rain must've got through while the loose slates were waggling about . . .

Oh, *what* a mess! More work for the job-creation boys. And who was going to pay for a new ceiling? *Poor* Mzz MacFarlane! The ceiling was even drooping above where she stood; and that little piece of wallpaper that she'd so often stuck back on was hanging off again.

She pushed at it tiredly, irritably. And with a whoosh another great section of wet plaster fell on her head. She gave a little scream of disgust and rage, clawing it away from her face so she could breathe. Now she'd have to wash her hair; *and* her T-shirt and jeans. Oh, she felt so *tired* . . .

So she almost missed it.

The great black beam that the fall of the ceiling had exposed. A funny rough beam, that hadn't been sawn or planed smooth; it was all dents and dimples, as if someone had tried to smooth it with an axe or knife.

And all along its edges there was funny old carving. Vines with leaves and bunches of grapes. Why do that to a beam that was going to be covered with a plaster ceiling, so that no one would ever see it?

Maybe it was older than the ceiling; maybe the

ceiling had been put over it afterwards? She had a sudden vision of Mr German saying that maybe the old monastery was inside the newer building . . .

Tired or not, she raced for the phone.

'Oh,' said Mr German. '*This'll* show them. This'll drive them *nuts*. Wait till the County Architect sees this. And the DOE. And the SPAB.' His voice was low, like he was in church. But it was full of joy and rage and . . . his eyes were wide and glowing in the gloom of the upstairs corridor, like he was Moses seeing the Burning Bush. He turned to Maggi, enclosing both her hands in his. She had an absurd idea he was about to go down on his knees before her, amongst all the filthy wet fallen plaster. 'Emmie, do you know what you've *done?*'

'I'm *Maggi*,' she said, a bit cross. '*What* have I done?'

'You've found the roofbeams of the monks' refectory. The only medieval refectory roofbeams that are still in place . . . and if the roof's still in place, the walls must also be the originals. Maggi, you've found half a medieval monastery that nobody dreamed was here. The monastery isn't hidden *inside* the house; it is the house; just covered up by later people. If we pull all the later stuff away . . .'

'Will that save the house for Mzz MacFarlane? It's the only place she has to live in . . .'

'Oh, money will be no object now. It'll all be restored. It'll take years. This is the greatest medieval find since . . .' His voice failed him. 'Goodness knows *what* we'll find. I must ring the County Architect.' He ran off downstairs, slipping and slithering through the wet plaster.

Maggi just stood there, in the semi-darkness of the top corridor.

'Well,' she said to the house. 'You're safe now. I hope you got what you wanted. Perhaps now you'll leave us *alone*!'

Another drip of water fell on her head. That was the only reply she got.

They left three mornings after. They were glad to leave. The place was no longer theirs. It belonged now to loud-voiced men with posh accents and expensive Range Rovers. It belonged to gangs of noisy students who pulled down great lumps of wall, even in Maggi's bedroom, even in the kitchen, doing far more damage than the job-creation boys had ever done. The walls were festooned with long lengths of red and white tape, and pinned-on bits of card with strange numbers like XXXIII/33. Then the local television crews moved in, and commentators waved their arms grandly, saying the same thing over and over again, to order.

Dad looked totally lost; Mzz MacFarlane looked

totally lost; even Mr German looked anxious and swept-aside. Only Percy and the twins made the most of it. Percy told of his battle with the fire brigade to any of the new people he could nobble; the twins jumped up and down in front of the telly cameras, pulling frightful faces.

They gathered in front of the *QE2* to say goodbye. Mzz MacFarlane still had her arm in a sling; but she held an enormous brown-paper parcel in her other hand. Maggi had a feeling, from the way she was holding it, that it must be a present for somebody. Probably Dad.

'Well, we'd best be off,' said Dad. 'There's no place for us here, now. Aah'm just a jobbing builder – ye've got plenty of clever beggars to help you now! You'll not be lonely!'

But Maggi wondered what Mzz MacFarlane would do at night, when all the clever beggars had gone.

Dad and Mzz MacFarlane looked at each other a long time. Then they gave each other a peck, cheek to cheek. 'Keep in touch,' said Dad.

'I'll drop you a postcard, to tell you the news,' said Mzz MacFarlane.

But that wasn't what they meant at all. They were like two people in a slow invisible earthquake, with a great gulf opening between them, and getting wider and wider. And Maggi knew who had made the gulf . . .

But the drowning face of Baz rose up, yet again, to quiet her guilty feelings. You had to look after your own. The house was quiet now, because it was getting what it wanted. But it was still dangerous.

'Right,' said Dad. 'C'mon, you two – into the back.' The twins shook hands shyly with Mzz MacFarlane, mumbled and were gone.

Now it was just Maggi and Mzz MacFarlane. She made herself look up into Mzz MacFarlane's eyes.

Mzz MacFarlane held out the huge brown-paper parcel.

'For me?'

'Old friends.'

Maggi tore open the parcel. Inside were the two teddy bears she had rescued from the bushes. Mended firmly and beautifully. Even the burnt bit had gone.

It was too much. She had probably ruined Mzz MacFarlane's life. And Mzz MacFarlane had still kept her promise about the bears.

'Thanks,' she mumbled, and fled into the cab of the *QE2*. She stuck the bears up on the deep dashboard, against the windscreen, so they could see where they were going. Then she waited.

Waited for the house to do something; to stop them escaping.

But the *QE2*'s engine started first time. And kept on going as they went down the drive for the last time. Percy waved from the lodge; and Wolf put back his great head and barked.

And still the *QE2*'s engine kept going.

Northwich.

Manchester.

The M62, and the long dry brown crawl over the Pennines, where something should've gone wrong, if anything was going on. But the engine's erratic song kept on, without a falter.

Huddersfield passed. Harrogate, full of posh shops, and of people who knew nothing about the abbey.

'Fancy a cuppa?' said Dad.

It was in the café that Maggi felt it. Felt the Abbey let go of her mind. One moment, as she toyed nervously with her cake, her mind was full of the Abbey. And the next, as she watched two kids trying to con their dad into buying them a bar of chocolate at the pay-kiosk, all thoughts of the Abbey left her. She found she couldn't think of the Abbey at all.

Another house took over. Home. 17 Brannen Street. Tiny. Scruffy, with three loose slates on the roof. The narrow hot terrace, with the men on the dole hanging around the front doors in their shirt-sleeves, smoking their last dog-ends. Doris Streeton.

And then she realized the most terrible truth. It

wasn't just the Abbey that held you prisoner. 17 Brannen Street did as well. Every house did, where you lived. The Abbey was a wild dangerous monster. And 17 Brannen Street was a monster that *bored* you to death.

But it was too late now. No more walking down corridors in the dark; no more smell of the rose garden. No more voices, calling . . .

Oh, Abbey, Abbey . . . she walked out of the café in despair.

There was a strange man standing by the *QE2*. A very Harrogate sort of man, with a light three-piece suit with a waistcoat, and a hat, and silver hair and a silver-topped walking-stick. A real old dandy. Nothing to do with *them*.

But he spoke to Dad in a very posh voice. He must be lost and asking the way. But no – he was tapping on the windscreen with an emphatic finger.

He was talking about *teddy bears*, for heaven's sake! And his voice was urgent.

'I swear they are genuine Stieff bears, sir – from 1902. They have the long arms and legs, and the correct coat of long-stranded plush, and the metal tag in their ears – and that characteristic square hump on their backs—'

Dad was staring at him, baffled, trying to work out whether he was a con man or a nutter. But Maggi had seen that kind of hand-sewn suit, that kind of wild enthusiasm before. They reminded her of Mr German.

The man grew even more frantic; produced a wallet and took a card from it; an ivory-coloured card with gold lettering and gold edge. He held it out, as if it was a key to a door, waggling it under Dad's nose and stating that he was H. Stanley Mountsetter of the firm of Christaby's, the world's premier auction house. Maggi took one look at Dad's face, and prayed that Dad wouldn't do anything hasty.

The twins were starting to snigger. Maggi saw her great last chance slipping away, and grabbed it.

'Let the gentleman see the bears, Dad,' she said in her firmest, most Mum-like voice. Instinctively, she added, 'Good manners don't cost anything.' That had been one of Mam's favourite sayings.

Dad, still bewildered, unlocked the van door, and passed out the bears one by one. H. Stanley Mountsetter of Christaby's, the world's most famous auction house, tilted the bears carefully, one ear against their fat worn stomachs. They made a dim oinking noise, which threw H. Stanley into fresh raptures. Then Maggi told him there were two more in the back of the van.

H. Stanley whirled them, people and bears, back into the café. Bought them fresh tea and fresh cream cakes. The twins dived in like the little pigs they were.

H. Stanley ordered more, and Maggi saw that with this vast expenditure on cakes, Dad realized H. Stanley *must* be serious.

'If you sell these,' said Dad, 'what kind of money we talkin' about?'

'It may surprise you, sir, but at auction – especially at our New York auction room – we are talking of a sum in the region of twelve or thirteen thousand dollars.'

Dad got a sort of glazed look. He just sat back warily, and let Maggi take over.

H. Stanley Mountsetter had departed, soothed by the reassurance that if the bears were ever to be sold, Christaby's would have first refusal. Maggi fingered the card gently, and stared at the four bears, who were now all sitting on the dashboard.

'Thirteen thousand dollars!' said Dad. 'How much is that?'

'About eight thousand pounds, I think, Dad.'

'Them Americans must be flipping bonkers.'

'Yes,' she said carefully. Dad stirred in his seat, uneasily.

'We can't keep them, pet. Mzz MacFarlane *needs* the money.'

'But she *gave* them to me!' Maggi tried to sound as indignant as she could. Which wasn't very.

'She didn't know what she was giving, pet. She just thought they were old useless things.'

'Yes,' said Maggi, gravely.

'We cannit post them back to her. They're too big, too valuable. They might get lost in the post.'

'Yes.'

'I think we'd best take them straight back to her now. I don't want the responsibility of them.'

The moment had come; the moment she had worked so hard for, this last hour. She knew if they went back now, they would never escape the Abbey again. Not if the Abbey could reach out *this* far, to pull them back.

And the bears . . . Mr Abbot . . . they were a gift the Abbey had given her. A kind of saying sorry, for almost drowning Baz. And she remembered the warm strong arm that had carried her back to safety when she was falling off the roof.

If you had to be the prisoner of something, it might as well be something exciting.

'OK,' she said. 'Let's go back.'

BREAK OF DARK

by Robert Westall

Is there a barrier dividing our everyday world from the dark unknown? If so, is it broken sometimes by alien creatures or by the dead returning?

Why else should three successive crews flying a Second World War bomber be driven to madness, despair, even to death, though the plane returns from each mission without a scratch? What is the mysterious smell in Roger and Biddy's house and what could account for the series of extraordinary thefts in Sergeant Nice's sleepy seaside town; surely the work of no human hand . . . ?

'Robert Westall is the father of the golden age of children's literature in this century, quite unrivalled in his sharpness of observation and pace of narrative . . . This book is always deeply engaging, a triumph of storytelling.'
Michael Morpurgo

DEFINITIONS
0 09 943953 0